RETRIBUTION

J.M. MADDEN

Cover by Octopi covers

Editing by MegEdits.com

❀ Created with Vellum

A NOTE FROM THE AUTHOR

The Dogs of War

If you haven't read the prequel, Genesis, book 1, Chaos, and book 2 Destruction, first, I STRONGLY suggest that you do. These books take place in a very short span of time and they are tightly woven together.

You can find links to every platform on my website JMMadden.com .

And PLEASE sign up for my newsletter! I very rarely bother you, only with truly important stuff.

www.jmmadden.com/newsletter/

CHAPTER ONE

Wulfe guided the Audi around the slow moving semi, then back into the left lane of traffic. Behind him, the air horn blared, but he didn't even care. If the semi was blocking traffic in the left lane he should expect to be passed on the right. He shook his head and lifted his foot from the gas pedal, wishing he was on the Autobahn. It was so freeing to have no limits other than your own fear and the capability of the machine you drove.

That was not this interstate, though. Sixty mile per hour speed limit felt like ... he could get out and walk faster. It definitely didn't suit him. He wanted to be in Arlington now, to find out why his contact had gone quiet. Anxiety churned in his stomach as he thought about everything that had gone on in the past two weeks.

They were on the verge of taking down the Silverstone Collaborative. Right now, Aiden was working with the Lost and Found Investigative Service and a team from the CIA to decipher the private notes they'd stolen from the research camp when they'd broken out two years ago. The information they'd discovered had helped Fontana rescue more than thirty prisoners from other research camps the company had still been operating.

Wulfe shook his head. The stupidity just astounded him. Was it an American thing?

Operations Officer Rose was point man for the investigation, and he was slowly and quietly beginning to bring in everyone named in Dr. Shu's covert information. Wulfe had just left D.C. where Rose had taken a former congressional intern into custody. The young man had been shocked and pale, but willing to talk about anything if it would keep him out of jail.

Wulfe wasn't sure what Rose was doing with everyone that he 'placed into protective custody' but they would reach a point where people were looking for those taken. The search warrant Rose had been granted by the federal judge was fairly sweeping, though, because this was a threat to national security. They'd thought that they would have a few days to get ready to take down Damon, but some plans were falling through. People, *parties of interest*, not being where they were supposed to be when teams went to apprehend them. Apparently minor details, but it spoke to a leak in the team somewhere. No team was one hundred percent secure, granted, but it seemed like there was some *group* actively working against their investigation.

Rose had a list of active targets he was working through and Wulfe decided to leave him to it. He'd been with them on several of the raids, using his enhanced senses to locate hidden dangers. So far, no one had been hurt in any of the incidents and he would like to think he'd played a part in keeping everyone safe. One of the names on the list had been a former Secret Service agent, and the man had been aware that something was going on when he'd gone to bed that night. His house had been staked out for hours and some in law enforcement or the military had a natural sense of danger that kept them alive. Harrison Granville had been one of those men, dangerous and aware, and when he'd 'gone to bed' he'd actually barricaded himself in the bedroom. It had taken Wulfe *finessing* his cooperation to de-escalate the situation to the point that Granville could be taken into custody without injury to anyone. Once they had the man in cuffs, they'd realized that Granville had been surrounded by weapons and homemade improvised explosive devices to protect his home or die trying. Though manipulating electricity wasn't Wulfe's greatest enhanced strength, he'd gone around the house and dismantled every single trap.

He was beyond tired and it was beginning to affect his ability to reason. He told Rose he was heading back to Arlington to recharge. Rose, just as tired as Wulfe, had given him an envious look. "Sleep for me a little."

Grinning, Wulfe had headed to his car.

The closer he headed toward the municipal center of Arlington, the more congested it got, and he was forced to throttle back. He would head to his flat first and check his computer and get a few hours of sleep, then he'd head out to surveil. He needed to find his informant. It was odd that she hadn't contacted him.

Wulfe scanned the area as he circled his building, looking for anything out of the ordinary. He wouldn't put it past Officer Rose to put a tail on him or have someone watching his place. Now that he and the other Dogs of War were a part of the CIA he supposed he needed to be prepared to assimilate. Or *cooperate,* at least. It had been a while since he'd been under anyone's control and just the thought of it set his teeth on edge. The German Navy had been the last time he'd been forced into strict adherence to regulations, and he had to admit, he didn't miss it at all. The CIA would have to give him the ability to act for himself. Rose had arranged U.S. citizenship for him as a part of his cooperation, though.

Circling around the block, he came in from behind the building, looking for anything out of the ordinary, but nothing drew his notice. Pulling into the underground garage he circled through the floors of parked cars. Again, nothing out of the ordinary. Swinging into a spot he pushed out of the seat and shut the door behind him. Keeping his head on a swivel he turned toward the elevator. It was already on the garage floor so the doors swished open. It took a minute to get to the top of the high-rise, so he took the time to expand his senses, feeling for spikes in energy. Nothing. Then he neared his floor and something brushed against his awareness. Not dangerous, exactly... it felt frantic.

Before the doors opened he pulled his HK, holding it to his side. There was one other penthouse on this floor, but the owner was rarely in it. It was an investment property.

The elevator doors dinged and swept open, but Wulfe didn't rush out. Instead he peered around the edge. Seeing who was waiting for him, he stepped out and secured the weapon in the holster at the base of his spine.

Elizabeth Wilkes rushed forward, her elegant hands outstretched. Tears streaked down her beautiful face and his gut clenched. "What's wrong?" he snarled.

Elizabeth's breath hitched in her throat. "Damon took him, Wulfe. He took my son."

———

The moment she spotted Wulfe stepping off the elevator, the fragile hold on her emotions broke. Elizabeth knew she was making a fool of herself, but she couldn't stem the tears. Her son was missing and her psychotic soon-to-be ex-husband was responsible.

Wulfe immediately stepped forward and cupped her face in his broad hands. "What has happened?"

Words began spewing from her mouth and she thought she made sense but he shook his head at her and turned her toward the door of his apartment. Keying in the code on the lock, he let her into the apartment then closed and locked the door behind them. She started to talk again but he shook his head and held up a hand. "Just a moment."

He drew a tall glass of water from the tap and guided her to one of the breakfast bar stools. "Drink. Then tell me."

Elizabeth did as she was told, and realized that the water quenched a thirst she hadn't even been aware of. "Thank you," she said, setting the glass on the marble counter.

Wulfe crossed his heavy arms over his chest and nodded at her. "Now, tell me. Slowly."

Elizabeth heaved a breath. "Damon hasn't been acting right since Mattingly was killed. They were lovers, I knew that," she said, lifting her chin, "but I didn't realize he was *in love* with her. It doesn't matter because our marriage was over long ago, but I thought he was above creating a public spectacle like he did. I've seen more devastation, more emotion from him in the past two weeks than in the past ten years."

She shook her head, crossing her arms beneath her breasts. "Then two nights ago something changed. I'm not sure what it was but all emotion shut down. I tried to talk to him about something and he was extremely distracted. Then Anton's intern, Lukas Evans, came out to the house for some reason, and when he left Damon *changed*."

Wulfe frowned, and his cold blue eyes shifted away. Elizabeth didn't like that. He knew something. "You have to tell me, Wulfe. Don't treat me like everyone else does around here."

His gaze met hers and softened. "Two nights ago there was a raid on a research camp— a Silverstone property— in Guyana. Twenty-three prisoners were rescued. Dustin Truckle was killed and Anton Scofield is in custody."

Elizabeth's mouth dropped open and she swayed in the chair, trying to assimilate all of the information he'd just given her. "My God," she breathed. "There were men in Guyana being tested on?"

Wulfe nodded once, staring at her hard. "They're not in great shape, but they will live. There were also a few survivors in a Brazilian camp."

She gasped and angry tears filled her eyes, but she forced them away. It seemed unbelievable. When Damon first told her about the testing program years ago, he'd made it sound like the men were all there voluntarily, of their own free will, and that it was over with now. It was only within the past six months that she'd realized that the men had been tested upon like animals. There had been documents she'd found in his home office. Reports that he'd received from Priscilla Mattingly when she'd been alive. Elizabeth had confronted Damon, and he'd given her empty words, telling her not to worry about the things that *men* needed to do to secure the futures for their families. Elizabeth had walked out of the room knowing that it was time to stop taking the easy road and letting Damon do everything. It was time to take control of her life, and her son's future.

Early in their marriage, she couldn't even pinpoint exactly when, she'd realized that she didn't even like Damon. It had been for her parent's sake she'd married him, and she'd regretted it almost immediately. She hadn't ever felt for him the way wives were supposed to feel. When she'd expressed her misgivings to her mother, Claudia had huffed in exasperation. That was when her mother had explained to her that there were times in a woman's life when she had to do things for the good of the entire family, regardless of her own personal feelings. And at the time, she'd felt she had no other choice.

Elizabeth had loved her parents, though she'd been

disheartened, and disillusioned. Had her parents' marriage been the same way? She wondered if her mother had ever mourned the loss of a true love, then married for the sake of the family.

It didn't matter. Elizabeth had made her bed, so to speak, years ago. She needed to focus on the present and what she needed to do *now*.

"I need more details," she told Wulfe firmly. "How did Truckle get killed? And where is Anton?"

Wulfe took the seat beside hers, propping his arms on the counter. "I'm not sure how much I'm allowed tell you," he said honestly.

Elizabeth reared back like she'd been slapped. He had the information, obviously, but refused to tell her? "After all this time," she breathed, looking away. Somehow this betrayal hurt more than any of the others, because Wulfe had always been in her corner. He'd never treated her the way everyone else thought they had a right to.

The change was shocking. More shocking, actually, than anything else that had happened recently. If he wasn't going to give her any information, then he probably wouldn't help her find her son, either. The despair that swamped her then was enough to drown her. Closing her eyes, she did everything she could to tamp down the panic trying to take her over. Panic wouldn't do anyone any good, especially her son. The longer they sat here not doing anything the further away her son could be traveling. Damon had vast resources, thanks to her. He could be heading to the end of the world right now, and she would be none the wiser.

Wulfe touched her shoulder, and she glanced at him. Taking a breath, she forced down the hurt. Her son needed her. "I understand why you don't want to get involved, but I have no one else to turn to. No one else has the resources to figure out where he's gone. You know things and can get things done."

"I never said I wouldn't help you," he growled, baritone voice rumbling. His German accent deepened when he was aggravated. His heavy black brows furrowed over his eyes. "I have to be careful though. Look at it from my position. We're in the middle of taking down a company that has been testing on servicemen from a dozen different countries, all financed by your husband. You've been married to him for many years, quietly working on your own projects in the background."

She scowled. "Are you seriously going to compare my endeavors with Damon's? I don't think we're anywhere near to the same playing field."

"Probably not," he agreed easily, "but from an outsider's perspective looking in, you were working at the company every day. You're on the board and listed as Director of Research. People will assume that you know everything that goes on there. Including the forced research with the Ayahuasca."

Elizabeth blinked, knowing he was probably right but not sure how to change that perception. The position that Damon had put her in was highly suspect, and she wondered if he hadn't been planning this for when it would all come crashing down around him. No, she didn't think he had any idea that things would fall apart like they had. He'd been too distracted recently.

"So, what *can* you tell me?" she asked finally. "Are all of the men you rescued going to survive?"

He frowned as if the question surprised him. "They should, yes. Some have injuries that will keep them in the hospital for weeks, maybe months, but they should all recover."

Again, he stared at her for a long moment, his dark blue eyes probing. "When is the last time you saw your son?"

Her throat tightened with emotion again. "Last night when I checked on him before bed. I kissed his cheek and told him to plug in his cell phone. He tends to use the thing until the battery is completely flat, which leaves it useless."

Wulfe nodded. "Then?"

"This morning I woke up and I thought he was just sleeping in a bit. His tennis teacher doesn't come until ten so I didn't begrudge him the extra time. Then Lukas called me. Damon wasn't answering his phone. I knew something was wrong, because he always answers his phone, even on the weekend. I went up to the bedrooms and I could tell there was stuff missing from the closets. There was cash taken from the safe in the master bedroom, and the game system Blake likes to play was gone from his console."

Wulfe scowled. "When could he have done this?"

Elizabeth looked away. "I assume early this morning. I sleep on the other side of the townhouse in the mother-in-law space. I dozed off on the couch and I didn't hear anything. All of his security men are gone, as well as Blake's personal guard."

Wulfe slipped off the stool and moved to stand at the expansive windows on the opposite side of the apartment. The city lit him from behind and she was struck with how big he looked. Protective. Strong. He had to help her because she had no one else.

CHAPTER TWO

Wulfe fought the frustration in his chest. Damon Wilkes was slime, he'd already known that. But to put a mother through this kind of worry... The idiot wouldn't hurt the boy, Wulfe knew that. But there was a chance he could use him as leverage.

As he looked out over Arlington, he spread his senses wide. Elizabeth was the brightest draw to his mental gaze, and he couldn't feel any subterfuge in her aura. Everything happened exactly the way she'd explained it.

Which left him with a problem. There was no way he couldn't help her find the boy, but he would have to talk to Aiden and Fontana, because this would be a huge potential hurdle for them. Helping the enemy, even slightly, could be a very hard pill for them to swallow. Focusing to the west, toward Denver and the Lost and Found offices, he tried to feel his compatriots, but they were too far apart. There was no way they could talk mind to mind like they'd become accustomed to over the past couple of weeks.

Running a hand through his hair, he forced away the exhaustion trying to drag him down. It had been thirty hours now with no sleep, and he was ready to crash. Then he looked at Elizabeth.

Normally, she was dressed the way the well-bred wife of a multibillion dollar company owner should be, with grace and style. Wulfe had never seen her with her pale blonde hair out of place, and her clothes perfectly pressed, but now, with her hair drawn haphazardly into a low ponytail, she didn't present the image he was used to. Her face was bare of makeup, yet surprisingly fresh. She looked very young and innocent, if it wasn't for the worry lines creasing her brow and mouth. And there was something flat in her brilliant blue eyes that made him worry.

He'd seen a similar expression in men that knew they were out of options. Elizabeth Wilkes was not a woman that normally had to worry like this.

"So, how do we find them? Are they carrying cell phones?"

She nodded, her hands folded in her lap. "I searched Blake's room, but he had to have taken it with him. The charger was still plugged into the wall, though so I don't know how long it will last."

Wulfe drew out his own cell-phone and pressed a number, sighing. Aiden Willingham answered on the third ring. "What's up, Wulfe?"

Wulfe looked at Elizabeth. "I'm in the middle of a situation, but I'm okay. Wilkes has bolted and I'm going to see if Rose can track his phone."

The silence stretched, as if Will could tell that there was more to the story that Wulfe wasn't willing to share, but he didn't press. "As far as I know he should be able to. The search warrant should cover it."

Yes, it should, but Aiden deserved to be apprised of what he was doing, as much as possible.

"I'll call him now. Fontana okay? And the survivors?"

Aiden sighed. "Fontana is buzzing. It's like getting the

men out of the camps has energized him or something. Or maybe it's the care Jordyn is giving him. He's been at her apartment for the past two days."

Wulfe chuckled, shaking his head. Fontana deserved to relax. He'd busted his ass over the past week.

"And how is your detective?"

Wulfe could almost hear the grin in his friend's voice. "Very fine." He cleared his throat. "Keep me posted on what you're doing if you can, and if you need us we can be there in a few hours."

"*Ja*, I know. Later."

Next he called Operations Officer Kevin Rose with the CIA.

"Wulfe," he grumbled, "you're supposed to be taking a break. Should have known you wouldn't give me a chance to catch my breath or sleep."

"You can sleep when you're dead. Isn't that the American saying? I need the location of a cell phone."

Rose sighed. "That takes a search warrant. It'll be a while before I can get that."

"It's Damon Wilkes' phone. He's turned rabbit. The current warrant should cover it."

"Fuck," Rose hissed. "Why haven't any of my men reported that?"

"I don't know, but he's gone. Been gone for hours according to my covert informant."

Wulfe allowed himself to look at Elizabeth, praying she wasn't making a fool of him.

———

Elizabeth understood the look, but she didn't know how to reassure him that she was telling the truth. They could go out to the house, but that wouldn't really mean anything. Her husband and son could be anywhere together. And according to the law nothing criminal had actually been committed yet. There was no law that said Damon had to report his every move to her.

If Blake didn't report for school in two days people would begin to ask questions. She was deathly afraid that they were already outside of the country. And if they were, she would have to have help from one of the most connected man she knew, Wulfe Terberger.

———

Blake didn't like the vibe he was getting on the plane. Something was up but he wasn't sure what. When he'd tried to ask his father, he'd been ordered to the back of the plane with his guard. Noah had guided him to a seat with a broad, implacable hand, and that had been the end of it.

Anger swirled in his belly. He was old enough to know what was going on. *Damn it.* Out of gut fear he looked around quickly. His mother would kill him if she ever heard him say any kind of cuss word. Even though she wasn't here he still felt guilty for even thinking it.

That was another thing strange about today. Dad had said that they were going to see his friend Cameron in Florida, but Mom normally went with them on these trips. The senator's wife really liked Mom, he thought.

Blake didn't understand why she wasn't here.

The odd things were adding up to something kinda scary.

He looked up at Noah. The man's face was like stone, no emotion showing whatsoever, earbuds parked in his ears. Blake was used to the way he looked when they were with the other guards. It was only when they were alone that his expression would ease. Noah was his friend and with a glance and the slightest of winks, Blake knew that Noah would tell him what he could when they were alone. It was kind of a system they'd worked out over the past couple years. Noah was this huge dude with a hard face. He had muscles bigger than Blake's leg, and veins running up and down his arms. He wore a black shirt with pockets, BDUs and his gun belt. Blake wasn't sure what kind of gun it was exactly, but something big to fit his massive hand. People looked at him then looked away as quick as they could, because Noah was that scary looking.

Noah had explained that it was kind of an honor to watch Blake, and he had to be the biggest badass of the group, otherwise one of the other men would try to take his spot.

Blake appreciated that Noah was his, because all of the other guards were idiots, some of them literally. They acted like they were big and bad, but Noah didn't let it affect him. Even when they called him names because of the night-dark color of his skin, he didn't let it bother him.

It made Blake mad, though. The guards were supposed to be protecting his father and mother, but it seemed like they were more interested in taking care of themselves and playing around. He'd seen them working out a few times, and he hadn't been impressed. Noah could kick all their butts together.

But then, Noah did a lot of things better than other men.

Looking out the window, he tried to figure out when they would be landing, but he hadn't really been watching the time. He reached for his phone, but Noah reached over and took it from his hand, setting it to silent. "Play with your tablet," he murmured, slipping the phone into his own pocket.

Blake wondered what the difference was, but he didn't argue. Reaching for his backpack he drew out his iPad. There was WiFi available so he logged on and started his game.

Like, ten hours later, his ears popped and he lifted his

head to look outside. They were still above the clouds but they must be coming in for a landing if his ears were feeling it. Mom normally gave him a stick of gum about this point.

"Do you have gum?" he whispered to Noah. Even though he had earbuds in, he always heard what Blake said.

The guard shook his head without looking at him.

Up in the front of the plane, his dad was leaning over and talking to his secretary, a grumpy old woman Blake had never liked. She was too... old. He'd overheard his mother saying that Ms. Heller had never married or had kids, and she was sad about that. Blake thought she was just a mean old lady.

His dad said she did a good job, though, so that was enough to keep her around. When they'd pulled up to the airport and he'd seen her waiting inside the plane, he'd been confused. It was Saturday. Yes, his dad would work on the weekend sometimes, but he'd never seen Ms. Heller anywhere other than at the office downtown.

Just another little thing that added up to weird.

Not sure why he did it, Blake angled his iPad to take a picture up through the middle of the seats. He'd gotten good at looking like he was playing his game and taking pics at the same time.

When they came in for a landing, he positioned the tablet to take a picture out the window. He recognized where they were. This was a neat airport because it was so close to the water, and sometimes when the pilot angled in for a landing he went out over the water to circle back, and you could see sharks in the water. Blake didn't see anything this time, just a calm blue, but he took a pic anyway. Miami was so different from Virginia.

They were met by several black Suburbans on the tarmac, and the senator's assistant, Miles, Blake thought his name was, met them. Something looked strange about Miles' forced smile, though. It was like he was angry and trying to smile through it. Or something. Miles held a hand out for his dad to get into one SUV, and motioned for Noah to take Blake to a second vehicle. Blake was happy to see that Dad's secretary stayed on the plane. Old cow.

Blake tried to meet his dad's gaze, and he thought about calling out to him, but he doubted he would even notice. Right now he seemed to be more worried about the black satchel he was carrying over his shoulder. The past couple of weeks his dad had been kind of distant, and he wondered if it wasn't because Ms. Mattingly had died.

That was one woman Blake didn't miss, wouldn't ever miss. She'd been so rude, sometimes even directly to his face. Actually, she'd been rude to everyone except his dad. And some of the things she'd said to Noah still made him furious. But Dad had considered her his best employee. The one time Blake had tried to tell him about the things she said, he'd been brushed off. As usual. Then he told his mom what Ms. Mattingly had been saying to Noah and when she got that "Mom is mad now" expression, he knew she'd take care of it.

Mom had spoken to Ms. Mattingly, and it had made the woman more cautious for a while, but only when Mom was nearby. The rest of the time she was even nastier. She made it very clear that he needed to stay out of her way or Noah was going to be looking for another job.

Blake didn't care what Mom said. Ms. Mattingly was a bitch. Well, had been.

He leaned forward in the seat to look out the window, but the seatbelt held him back. Didn't matter. He'd seen it before. The senator's estate was beautiful and cold, literally. It seemed like they always had the AC set on the super-cold tundra setting. And in the huge stone mansion, it seemed like everything stayed cold, in spite of the Florida sunshine.

"When are we going back to Virginia?" he asked, glancing at Noah.

The big man glanced at the other guards in the car. "Not sure. You'll have to ask your father."

Blake didn't like that answer. Noah always knew everything. He said he heard whispers a lot. But maybe he didn't want to say with the senator's security here.

Blake waited until they were in the guest room, just he and Noah, before he asked again.

"I'm not sure, Blake," Noah told him, standing at the window with his hands on his hips. "Things are a little weird right now."

That answer made him more worried than anything else that had happened that day.

CHAPTER THREE

When Wulfe looked at her with that heavy frown on his face, she knew she wasn't going to like what he said.

"It will take a while to track them down. He has to have a warrant to run a check on the cell phone. While he's doing that, we both need to take a bit to calm down."

He crossed to the kitchen and got her another drink of water, then one for himself as well. There were deep furrows around his mouth and eyes. For the first time she realized how tired he looked. Her conscience twinged.

"I'm sorry, Wulfe. I just didn't know who to go to."

"I know, Elizabeth. It's okay. You needed to come to me. There's just a lot going on right now and I haven't slept for over thirty hours. I'm not operating at peak performance."

Her eyes widened with understanding. "I'm even sorrier then. When will we hear back from whomever you called?"

Frowning, he gave a single shake of his head. "Not sure. He's... busy right this second."

Elizabeth looked around the apartment. "Why don't you go lie down for a while, then? I'll wait here, if you don't mind.

Then, when you do hear, we can be ready to go. I have a bag with me and everything."

Wulfe stared at her unflinchingly for a long moment and she wondered what he was thinking. He had such an implacable face. Eventually, he gave a single nod. "I think that would be wise. Make yourself at home. I haven't been here for a while but there should be some food in the fridge and cupboard. Remotes are there." He pointed to the glass coffee table sitting in front of the mocha leather sectional. "If I can get a few hours, I'll be ready to fight."

She winced, seriously hoping it wouldn't come to that. "I'll be here. Go sleep. I'll be fine."

Without another word he turned and headed down the hallway to the bedroom.

Elizabeth looked around the beautifully appointed but impersonal apartment and wanted to scream. Sitting on her behind was going to drive her insane when she had no idea where her son was, but she needed Wulfe at peak performance. She felt a flush roll across her face as the words crossed her mind. It was totally inappropriate to be thinking about his attractiveness at a time like this, but she couldn't help it. It had been weeks since she'd seen him.

Other things had been on her mind as well though. Like the testing that Damon had approved.

When she'd first seen Wulfe standing on the corner in front of Silverstone Collaborative all those months ago, she'd thought she was seeing a ghost. It was a good thing she'd had a driver that day because she had watched him for several long seconds. Their eyes had met and he had turned so that he was continually facing the car as it rounded the corner, then went down into the parking garage. He had wanted her to see him.

That day—week— had been a total fog. She'd debated contacting his family in Germany to see if she could talk to him, or trying to track him through the German Navy. Instead, she'd waited, just on the off chance that she'd been seeing things that day.

The following week he'd approached her at a coffee shop. Seeing him had been... enthralling. The handsome young sailor in his sharp German Navy uniform had matured into an equally intense, handsome man, standing head and shoulders above everyone else in the shop. It had taken her a minute to understand that he was speaking to her, telling her that she needed to look into the Spartan program.

"I'm sorry, what?"

"The Spartan Program. Your husband has been financing illegal drug testing on soldiers using a derivative of the Ayahuasca plant. The drug is supposed to create super soldiers by releasing chemical inhibitions in their minds and bodies, then putting them through aggressive testing. Men have been maimed and killed. Dr. Shu was heading the program."

That name rang a bell. "Are you sure?"

He stared at her for a long moment as people swirled around them. "Yes, I was one of the men they tested it on."

Before she could say or do anything he was gone, leaving her wondering which of them was the crazy one.

At first she'd dismissed what he'd said as fiction. Then, little things began to prick at her, things she'd seen or heard that had appeared odd to her. As one of the doctors in the research program as well as the owner of the company, she had complete access to the computers and she'd been able to explore. She hadn't found anything about a Spartan project, though. Not until, a few weeks later, she let herself into Damon's office when he'd been at a business dinner and logged onto his computer. It had all been there; the countries helping them, where the money was going, but no reports on results that she could find. That set her onto a path to find out about the men. She'd never found a complete file, just a few mentions about the tests themselves.

Wulfe had called her occasionally, prodding her to look for certain things, but more often than not she'd hit dead ends. Once she'd told him what she'd found, or not found, he'd hung up. He hadn't seemed to want to connect on a personal level at all.

That was fine. She'd understood. He'd given her the address of this place, one of his brother's homes, and told her to only come here if it was a true emergency. This was definitely an emergency.

Pulling her cell phone from her pocket she checked for messages. Nothing. Setting her phone on the counter she wandered through the kitchen, getting things together for a cup of tea. Wulfe, or his brother, had an assortment of herbal teas in one cupboard. With the tea steeping in a cup, she curled up on the end of the sectional and set her cup beside her. There was a book about whales on the table beside her, so she picked it up and started flipping through it.

Before she knew it her eyes were drifting shut.

Elizabeth jerked awake to a subtle notification from her phone. Grabbing it up, she looked for the text. No text, just another email. She was on the verge of dropping the phone to the couch beside her when something made her swipe through and open the email. It was from Blake's Gmail account.

Mom, what are you doing? Why didn't you come with us to the senators house? I thought you like Mrs. Hall. Look at this. They've got security dogs patrolling the grounds now. Look at this one, isn't he beautiful? I wasn't supposed to mess with him, but he likes me.

Noah took my phone but I don't know why. I'll call you when I get it back.

Attached to the email was a beautiful, close-up picture of

a big black dog sitting way too close to her smiling son and baring his very sharp looking teeth at the camera.

She let out a little sob as she reread the email. It told her so much. She glanced at the time in the corner of her display. It was after four p.m. She and Wulfe had been sleeping for hours. Pushing up from the couch, she jogged down the hallway to the far bedroom and pushed open the cracked door.

Then she went still, completely mesmerized. Wulfe slept on his front, his bare, beautiful ass exposed to the air of the bedroom. He was sprawled diagonally across the king-sized bed and she was amazed at how much space he took up. That same space would accommodate six of her.

Then she realized his body was sheened with sweat in the cool room, and the muscles of his back were tense. She crept toward the bed, unsure what to do.

"Wulfe?" Reaching out a hand she touched his bare shoulder.

Immediately, he sprang from the bed, quicker than she could believe he could move. One second was flat on his face, and the next he was across the room, staring at her with his fists raised in front of him. Muscles bulged in his chest and abdomen, and his knees were bent like he was going to be attacked. Elizabeth blinked and snapped her mouth shut, wondering if she'd seen what she thought she had. No one moved that fast. Maybe she was still waking up. Then she saw the expression in his eyes, and her heart broke for him. "I'm sorry," she said clearly. "I should have knocked. Are you okay?"

He blinked at her, his midnight blue eyes even darker than normal. The short black hair on his temples was damp with sweat. "*Ja. Es get mir gut, danke.*"

Did he even realize he'd answered her in German? She

didn't think so. "Blake emailed me. I'll tell you about it after you get dressed."

That damn flush swept over her cheeks again and she turned for the bedroom door. She kept her eyes directly ahead as she swept out, but her peripheral vision worked just fine.

When Wulfe stepped into the room a few minutes later, his eyes were guarded. "What did the email say?"

Obviously he wanted no mention of the scene in the bedroom. That suited her just fine. "He said he's at the senator's house in Miami. I assume he means Cameron Hall. He's been Damon's number one supporter in the Senate. Cameron has had us to his house several times socially."

Wulfe was already on his phone, typing a text message it looked like. Elizabeth waited, wondering what their next move was. It would take hours to get down there and there was a very good possibility that Damon and Blake would be gone by the time they got there.

Finally, Wulfe looked at her, "I have a plane waiting at the airport for us, but I'm waiting for a call back. We need to make sure that's where he is before we get in the air and have no cell service."

His phone rang in his hand. "Yes?"

Elizabeth watched as he turned away, toward the windows. He murmured softly, as if he didn't want her to hear, and that stung. She understood that she was technically standing on the wrong side of the morality line right now, but it wasn't a position she chose deliberately. The Silverstone Collaborative was her family legacy. The Cole family had been in business for almost a hundred years and had developed dozens of patented lifesaving drugs. She had degrees in business management and a doctorate in research medicine but when the time came for her father to retire, his own daughter had not been his first pick. At the time he'd claimed it was because she was so young but she knew that was a lie. Daddy convinced her that marriage would be ideal. Damon Wilkes, a friend of the family who had just completed a business program, could run the business and make them money and she could back the medical research side of it. Daddy had taken an advisory position to guide Damon until his death a few years later.

Elizabeth shook her head at herself. God, she'd been naïve. No, she'd been stupid. But at the time she'd been in a crisis without anyone else looking out for her best interests, and she hadn't known what to do.

Wulfe turned around and nodded to her, and Elizabeth's emotions began to hum. They would be flying to Florida and not a moment too soon, as far as she was concerned.

"We'll meet you at the airport," he said into the phone, and hung up.

Elizabeth wondered who exactly it was they would be meeting. She assumed someone in the CIA. This would probably be their kind of gig, but she would wait for him to confirm. After everything Damon had done, she was more than willing to testify against him in any way possible.

After she retrieved her son.

"Damon is definitely in Florida," Wulfe told her, turning back. "Satellite images picked him up exiting the plane, along with half a dozen guards and a young boy."

Her heart jumped in her chest. "We need to get down there."

"Yes, though I'm not sure yet how we're going to proceed. Do you need to take anything with you?"

She grabbed her laptop, purse, and overnight bag, and slipped her phone into her pocket. "I'm ready."

Wulfe sent off a couple of text messages, then got ready to leave. Within just a few minutes he was escorting her onto the elevator and down to the parking garage. She didn't recognize the imported sports car he directed her to, but it didn't matter. She slid into the vehicle and drew the belt across herself. She'd driven with Wulfe before.

They sped out of the parking garage and onto the street to a chorus of honking horns. Elizabeth clutched at the door and the center console, but Wulfe seemed nonchalant. Excited, even. His eyes were sparkling and there was a hint of excitement in his expression.

Elizabeth was excited too, because things were finally starting to happen. For months— no, *years*— she'd bitten her tongue and tried to be the good little wife, but it was time she stood up for herself and her son. Now that Wulfe was involved things would be happening, and she was going to stand up for her happiness.

CHAPTER FOUR

Officer Kevin Rose's tired brown eyes widened when Wulfe and Elizabeth crossed the tarmac toward the CIA plane. It would have been funny if they weren't in such a dire situation.

No one—not the other Dogs of War, no one at Lost and Found, and certainly no one at the CIA—had known that Elizabeth Wilkes was his informant.

True surprise showed in the officer's expression as he held out a hand to Elizabeth. "Mrs. Wilkes, I'm sorry to meet you under these circumstances. But I want you to know on behalf of the U.S. Government, we appreciate what you've done in helping us to bring your husband and his conspirators to justice."

"It's a pleasure to meet you as well, Officer Rose. And I don't feel like I've done enough. Those men should have never been in those camps."

He sighed as he followed her into the plane. "I'm not going to argue with you there, but we're going to do what we can now to make sure everything is right, now. Because they deserve it."

"I agree." She told him, moving to a set of leather seats. "We need to sit down and talk about what part the company itself is going to play in this mess. I've made some changes that are going to kick into effect within a few days, and I want you to know that the Silverstone Collaborative will be covering the cost of care for every single one of those men."

Rose settled into the chair beside Elizabeth, Wulfe took one of the ones facing them, strapping the belt across his waist. Rose glanced at him, a skeptical look on his face, before turning back to look at Elizabeth.

The insecure, worried mother was gone. In her place was a competent, poised, professional woman talking to a representative of the U.S. Government. Wulfe appreciated the metamorphosis. *This* was the Elizabeth that was going to have to change the future of the company. This was the woman that was going to have to carry it through the rocky times ahead, because she knew that there was a very real possibility that the federal prosecutor would file charges against her husband, and possibly even her. As much as he hated to admit it, Wulfe hoped that that would not happen. He had a monster hard-on against the company, he would admit that, but not if she was running it. He would make sure he would do everything in his power to make sure it didn't happen, but his influence here in the States wasn't what it was in Germany.

Over the past few months she had helped him out several times. Just little mentions here and there of people that had been in the offices, or requisitions she'd seen that had appeared odd. Nothing groundbreaking but enough to make him hope that she was not involved with the program.

Because as much as he tried to fight it, he'd begun to soften toward her.

"I have to admit, ma'am, that I didn't expect you to be the

informant," Rose told her, crossing an ankle over his knee as the plane took off.

Eight other agents had trooped onto the plane as well and settled at the back. They'd left a bit of a privacy cushion around the three of them, which Wulfe appreciated. This initial conversation was going to be very important.

Elizabeth glanced at Wulfe, and he felt the impact of it in his gut. "Wulfe and I were an item many years ago, before I married. When he came to me with questions about a few things the company had done, I began to dig. And I didn't like what I found. I couldn't *not* help him then."

Rose nodded, watching her carefully. "Let me be blunt, Mrs. Wilkes."

"Please," she said, crossing her legs as the plane leveled off.

"You realize that as integral as you are to the company, not many people will believe that you didn't know what was going on beneath your nose. Quite possibly, the federal prosecutor chief among them."

Wulfe frowned at the echo of his own thoughts. Elizabeth lifted her delicate chin, her pale blue eyes steady. "I am very aware of that, Officer Rose, and if the prosecutor wants to file charges against me, I will accept the consequences for being a part of the company. Yes, I was blithely ignorant of the direction Damon had taken. I'm happiest in the lab, working on my own projects. But I should have kept a better eye on things. That's my fault. I know charges are a possibility, even the dismantling of my company. But until then, I am going to do everything in my power to make sure that Damon Wilkes is brought to justice and my son is brought home safely. And I will make every part of my life and business as transparent as possible."

Rose glanced at him and Wulfe couldn't read his expression, but he could read the approval in the man's aura. Rose wouldn't flat out tell her that he liked what she said, but if she could get him into her corner he could sway the federal prosecutor one way or the other.

"Well, we'll appreciate any information you can give us, obviously. And we'll do our best to get your son back to you."

For a moment her eyes glimmered with tears, but she pushed them back. "Thank you for that, Officer Rose."

Wulfe wished he could give her the comfort that she needed. Elizabeth had been standing alone for so long.

"You mentioned changes happening in the next few days?"

Elizabeth gave a single nod. "I've called a meeting of the board for Monday morning. I've appointed myself acting head of Silverstone Collaborative. Damon's personal and professional behavior over the past two weeks have cemented my resolve to take over the company. Even before this hare-brained kidnapping I planned on booting him to the curb. He has been served divorce papers, though he hasn't signed them. I thought he'd gotten some whisper of my ousting him from one of the board members which compelled him to act but Wulfe told me about the raid in Guyana. I think he feels the world is coming down on him. I'm going to help him out the door."

Wulfe gaped at her, amazed at her actions. Rose seemed to be as well. "You realize that this could put you even more into the line of fire. If this situation goes public…"

"I have a team working on worst case scenarios and media relations. They don't have exact details, but I gave them a hypothetical situation to prepare for." She glanced between the two men. "I'm well aware this puts me on the front lines, but we have to make this right. My family's company has always worked for the betterment of humanity. But there's no spinning this. We messed up, horribly, and now we're going to have to pay for it however we need to."

Wulfe gave her a slight smile, unbelievably proud of her.

The smile seemed to shock Elizabeth because she lost her bravado. She turned her head and looked out the window, obviously trying to regain her composure.

"Will the board agree with the move?"

"It doesn't matter if they do or not," she said with a slight smile. "Silverstone is still a private company. They are there for guidance only. And since my parents have both died, *I* have the final say. My son owns a portion of the company as well."

Interesting. So because her family owned the company she could basically walk in and tell them what was going to happen. What was it Fontana said the other day? Balls? Baller? Wulfe was very familiar with company dynamics like this. His brother had built a software company with a box of computer parts in a spare room, and was now a millionaire many times over, if not more. Wulfe had supported him from the beginning, and backed his move *not* to take over the family investments. They let a very capable firm of investment managers do that, and Nikolas was able to do what he wanted. The family wasn't especially happy. They came from a long line of German aristocrats and the oldest son was *always* the head of the family. After their father died it was expected that he would take over the reins. Nik had refused, though, and forced the more minor cousins— bloodsuckers who had no goal in life other than to live off of the family money, out of the family *Herrenhaus* located outside of Berlin.

It had been a shock to everyone, but Nik had stood firm.

As he looked at Elizabeth now, he could see the same determination he'd seen in Nik's eyes years ago. She'd matured a lot in the ten years since he'd seen her.

"Well, then, if you don't mind, this might be an ideal time to do an official interview."

Mouth tightening, Elizabeth nodded her assent. Rose waved a woman up from the back of the plane and several people shifted. Wulfe was asked to give up his seat, but he refused. The woman seemed shocked that he wouldn't do what she needed and scowled at him, but Wulfe merely smiled. He would stay right here to give Elizabeth the support she needed.

Elizabeth caught his refusal and she gave him a slight nod of her head in appreciation.

For two hours straight, three CIA officers questioned Elizabeth about every aspect of the company, her marriage, her money, and her son. When she wasn't clear on a subject she drew out her laptop and began digging through company documentation. Wulfe was shocked to learn that Elizabeth was the actual owner of the company, not Elizabeth *and* Damon. Damon owned nothing in the marriage, other than the gifts that Elizabeth had given him at the beginning of the marriage. Literally, every cent the company made was Cole family money. Damon's personal income was his salary, nothing more. Granted, it was a robust salary, but nothing compared to the family wealth.

He was also shocked to learn that she had filed for divorce six months ago, but Damon had refused to sign the paperwork. Their lawyers were trying to work out a settlement. There was a prenuptial agreement in place, but Damon was trying to fight it.

"Why six months ago?" he asked curiously.

The agents also seemed interested in her answer, heads swiveling to her.

Elizabeth blinked and looked down at her folded hands for a moment, before lifting her gaze to his. "Because six months ago I learned about the testing that had taken place on the men in those camps."

Wulfe felt his heart stutter in his chest, and his body warmed. Six months ago, almost to the day, he'd spoken to her for the first time in ten years.

Once the Dogs of War escaped the torture camp two years ago, they decided on a plan of action and split the information they'd stolen between them and scattered. Once Wulfe had hidden his, it had been his job to watch the Silverstone Collaborative and the principals to gather any kind of dirt possible. Elizabeth had drawn his attention more than any other. How could she not? They'd had a brilliant, burning, star-crossed affair— the pampered little pharmaceutical heiress and the German sailor. He'd attended parties with his father in Washington. At that time the Silverstone Collaborative was run by her father, Anson Cole, and they'd just begun to work with the federal government creating immunizations for the homeless.

His own father, Fredrik Terberger, was an industrialist and a titled German aristocrat, and he'd been working with the U.S. on several overseas projects. The Terberger name traced back to medieval German royalty, and Wulfe remembered how his father used to get off on that, silently lording it over everyone, even the highest ranking American politicians. They would talk business at the parties and as soon as he was in private, he would mock everyone he'd talked to that night. Wulfe and his brother Nik had been a part of his retinue. They'd both been in the Navy then and they made a striking, powerful image in their dress uniforms. The Navy had given them special dispensation to accompany their father on these trips because it was so important to the German economy. Attending those parties had taught them business and political strategy, but also soured them on the entire process. It became the most loathed part of their military careers.

Then they'd attended a party for the National Institutes of Health, and Anson Cole and his daughter had been there. At first, Wulfe hadn't even noticed the young girl standing just behind Mr. Cole because she'd blended in so well, then she'd glanced up and he'd seen the ice blue of her eyes set in her beautiful young face. They were introduced and he remembered bowing over her hand, which made her blush, but that was all he remembered of that meeting. Well, that and the rush of heat every time he remembered her. Elizabeth was only a few years younger than he was—older than he'd thought—but there'd been an innocence to her that he'd lost many years ago.

They'd seen each other several times over the following months and he'd liked her more every time they'd spoken. But when he'd finally asked her on a date, she'd told him a flat no, leaving him speechless. He'd been so sure of himself.

"Why?" he'd demanded finally.

Elizabeth had given him a sad smile. "Because if I date you I'm going to fall in love with you. And with you in Germany and me here, it just won't work between us. Besides, our families won't allow it."

The smile had faded from her eyes and he didn't like the solemnity that took its place. She spoke the truth, though; neither one of them were free to live their lives as they wanted. They were both constrained by family expectations. Glancing around the terrace where they were hidden, he'd stepped closer to her, cupping her face in his hands. Then he'd kissed her, as sweetly and carefully as possible. Wulfe would always remember the incredible taste of her innocence, as if it were her first kiss. Even now, years later, he remembered the feel of her lips trembling beneath his own. The sweet taste of her breath as she panted into his mouth. The shudder that rippled through her slim body.

In spite of her misgivings she'd accepted his offer of a date for the next night, and they'd had a wonderful time. It had ended in another kiss, even more thrilling than the last. It seemed that within days he was begging his brother to help him with a place they could get away from both families.

Nikolas rented a small, furnished apartment outside of D.C. and it had been an oasis to them. They fell in love.

Then, just as she'd expected, their families had learned of their affair. He'd been recalled to Germany within hours and she was taken home by family security.

He'd tried to keep in touch, but it had been too hard. At one point his father had told him that her family was pressuring her to marry. They had the perfect man in mind, too, they said, and it wasn't Wulfe. He'd gotten one call through to her, asking for an explanation. She'd sobbed as she'd told him she would love him forever, but that family had to come first. Their love had been a brilliant thing and she would remember him always.

He'd believed her, until he'd discovered that the Silverstone Collaborative, her family's company, had been the one to conduct the abusive Ayahuasca training on them. Wulfe had a sneaking suspicion that her father had a hand in his drafting into the program, as well, but there was no way he'd ever be able to prove it now.

Wulfe blinked away the past. It had all happened years ago, but he knew, as he looked at her now, that they could take up right where they left off if she gave him the chance.

CHAPTER FIVE

E lizabeth was glad when the interrogation was over. That had taken a lot out of her. Her emotions were buzzing, hypersensitive. The beginning of a migraine pressed at her eyes and she let her head fall forward so that she could massage her temples. Rose and his people had moved to the back of the plane, but she could still feel their attention on her. She knew that every move she made would be under intense scrutiny. If she were in their shoes she would be doing the same thing.

"Are you okay?"

"Yes," she said, without looking up. Part of the reason she was getting the migraine was because of the brightness flashing in through the plane windows. If she could keep her head down for a while there was a chance she could head it off.

"Elizabeth, what's wrong?"

Lifting her head, she forced a smile for Wulfe. "Just a headache, is all."

Immediately Wulfe pushed out of his seat and walked toward the front of the plane. There was a small area with a fridge and coffee station, and a lavatory on the opposite side. She watched as he began rummaging through latched compartments as if he owned the plane. Finally, he found what he was looking for and returned to her. He handed her a packet of Advil and a can of Diet Coke. He even had the courtesy to open the Coke for her while she ripped open the packet of pills.

"Thank you, Wulfe."

Tipping back her head, she swallowed the pills and chased them with the soda. It warmed her heart that he seemed to remember what to do for her headaches. Wulfe had always been thoughtful that way.

"I'm sorry you had to go through that," he told her, tipping his strong chin toward the back of the plane.

Elizabeth shrugged. "I knew I would at some point. As soon as I started helping you I knew I was making a choice I would have to pay for later. And I am, in many different ways."

She forced a smile, hoping that he wouldn't read too much into that. "Don't worry about me. I'm tougher than you think."

"I don't know. You were pretty strong years ago."

Elizabeth made a face. "Definitely not. Everyone ran my life but me. Heck, even the maid had more clout in my house than I did. I was just the pretty little purebred trinket to be married off."

Wulfe looked thoughtful, and he took a moment to respond. "I know it seemed that way to you, but we had very similar lives. I wasn't allowed to grow in my own direction either."

"True." Her expression softened. "I know you didn't always get along with him, but I thought about you when your father died. I'm sorry I couldn't be there for you."

That was the understatement of understatements. By that

time she'd been married to Damon for seven hellish years. Her son was the brightest part of her life, as well as her work at the company.

Wulfe shrugged, his broad shoulders spanning the seat. "We weren't close. Especially since he was the one to send me into the research program."

Her mouth dropped open. "Are you serious?"

He nodded. "My brother discovered paperwork in my father's personal safe. He thought that a little 'enhancement' would do the family name good and he was more than happy to use me as the guinea pig. We never got along. There was a contract in the safe, signed by your husband, that guaranteed my father first option if the serum was a success. My father actually invested heavily in a small pharmaceutical company in Germany in the expectation that he would be able to produce it there."

She gaped, stunned at the cold-bloodedness of the entire mess. She felt her own situation pale in comparison.

"I'm so sorry, Wulfe." Leaning forward in her chair she rested her hand on his as her eyes filled with tears. "If I had known I would have done something. I swear that to you."

His jaw tightened and his eyes met hers. She could feel how much it hurt him that his own family had handed him over. He looked down at their touching hands, turning his own palm up to curl his fingers over hers. "I know you would have, Liz. That makes some of the pain in my heart ease."

Her eyes closed at the shortened version of her name. He had been the only one to ever use it. He'd been the only one she'd ever *allowed* to use it.

"Your brother looked for you, right?"

Wulfe shrugged lightly. "When the German Navy tells you that your brother died in a training exercise, and sends you back a box of ashes, you tend not to question that too much. It's the way of our military, and even our family. Many generations of Terbergers have served and died for *Deutschland*. I was a younger son, so it wasn't unexpected."

Elizabeth frowned, running her thumb over a couple of his fingers. It was very nice to hold his hand this way. Though if the CIA officers noticed... she shut that thread off. What did she care if they did notice? She was divorcing her reprehensible husband. With any luck, when the CIA got their hands on him they would put him away for the rest of his life.

It would be up to her to pick up the pieces of their life. She'd taken steps to do that, but she hoped they'd been the correct steps.

Elizabeth looked down at their linked hands, a little shocked at the intimacy. They'd crossed a barrier in the past few hours, and she loved that he was allowing her touch. But, if her future was going to be secure, she needed to make sure she did it on her own. Leaning back in the chair, she gently withdrew her hand from Wulfe's. Something like hurt flared in his eyes before he glanced away. When his gaze met hers again, it was cool and steady, as if the hurt had never been there. How many times had he been wounded by those he was supposed to be able to depend upon?

"What's the plan when we get there?"

"Not sure," he murmured. "Rose hasn't said."

Elizabeth sighed. Nothing like walking into a situation blind. If it was up to her she'd just go in there, find Blake and walk out, no niceties or politeness. The thought that Cameron Hall backed the testing on the men and hid what they were doing from the U.S. Government, disgusted her. The fact that her son was on his heavily guarded estate terrified her. He could be used as leverage, or just killed outright. If Hall was as dirty as she thought there was no limit to the lengths he'd go to in order to protect his career and future.

She needed to think of something else before she had panic attack.

"So," she murmured, voice rough, "now that the CIA has bled me dry can you tell me more about the men that were rescued? And how Anton was involved?"

Wulfe stared at her for several seconds before giving her a single nod. "When Priscilla Mattingly died she left a power vacuum in the company. You were aware of that." Elizabeth nodded. "No one knew exactly the extent of what she did. From what we've gathered, Anton tried to take over her duties, but things were slipping through the cracks. Dustin Truckle was next in the chain of command. Damon assigned Truckle to take over Mattingly's duties, but apparently Anton did not agree with the situation. He thought if he could be on-site, managing, he could pull things together. It was a matter of perfect timing that everything fell together the way it did."

Wulfe scrubbed his bristled chin with his hand. "Five days ago we sent a team in to visually check all of the camps Dr. Edgar Shu had listed in his notes. The first camp was uninhabited, but there is a mass grave that the CIA is excavating. Human remains have been found there and most of the ones that have been identified are American. The second camp, in Brazil, held a few prisoners. They were in the process of being moved out to the third camp when Fontana's team inserted and pulled out those survivors. They'll recover."

Elizabeth realized she was shaking her head, as if she could choose not to hear what he was telling her. "What had they been doing? Can you tell me specifically?"

"One gentleman they pulled out had a large swath of skin removed from his stomach. It was exposed to the jungle air as well as everything around him, dirt, insects, and weather. There was also one female survivor in the camp, but we don't think she was actually in the program. Right now we think she was being held captive by one of the guards."

Elizabeth flinched. "Are you serious?"

Wulfe nodded. "Last I heard she was responding well to treatment, but she'll have a long way to go."

She cringed in spite of herself. "And the others?"

"There was a variety of injuries. Amputations, several bone injuries. They're still figuring out all of the illnesses they've been injected with."

Elizabeth wanted to cry. All this time...

Then an even more horrifying thought hit her. Her eyes drifted up to Wulfe's, and he seemed to understand what she was asking because he shook his head. "Not now."

She was chastened. Torture wasn't something he would want to talk about within earshot of the CIA. "I'm so very sorry, Wulfe."

He turned his head to look out the small window, and they didn't say anything the rest of the flight.

———

They flew into a small, private airstrip just west of Miami. They could drive to the senator's beach house estate from here.

They didn't though. Instead they went to a different house and just waited. It was obvious this was some kind of CIA safe house. Big, pretty, very Florida, obviously used to belong to a drug dealer or something. There were padlocks on every... single... door... She looked around, curious.

"Do you lock people in their rooms?" she asked Officer Rose.

He gifted her with a roguish smile. "Only if they're really bad."

The flash of humor in the normally staid man's voice made her smile slightly.

As soon as they'd touched down she'd checked her email

for anything new from her son, but there was nothing. "Do you think I should email him back?" she asked Wulfe.

He thought about the question for a moment. "Better not yet. Don't want him to act before we're ready."

Rose agreed, so it left her waiting. Again.

There were no texts from Damon either. She'd sent him a dozen messages but he hadn't responded to any of them.

"What will the motivator be to actually do something?" she asked, crossing her arms beneath her breasts.

Rose gave her a one-shouldered shrug. "Not sure. We know where he is now so my men are going to stake out the house and see what goes on."

Which left her exactly nowhere. In desperation she got on her computer. Maybe if she had more evidence against Damon she could sail the company out of these dire straits.

CHAPTER SIX

Noah glanced out over the balcony, sending his senses wide, his enhanced hearing filtering out the useless buzz from the information he could actually use.

There were a few guards in the kitchen, generally making themselves nuisances. It sounded like Gonzalez, Maker, and Adams from his team. They were all assholes. The cook, who sounded like an older gentleman, was frazzled, snapping orders at someone to move her ass. The guards were demanding to be fed and the cook very eloquently told them they could go fuck themselves. He had better things to do.

Two of the senator's guards at the front door were murmuring softly to each other. They were pissed that Noah's team had come in like they owned the place. Alpha male anxiety thrummed between the two men. They were battle buddies, so to speak, and they felt like their territory was under siege. They were debating options on how to get rid of the invading team. "It won't be an issue after tomorrow," one of them said, then they were both silent. Noah wondered what was going to happen tomorrow.

Then, in the study on the lower floor and to the east, he

heard Senator Cameron Hall and Damon Wilkes talking. He recognized their voices immediately, Damon's smooth charm and the Senator's confident drawl.

"It's not as bad as all that, Damon," the senator said, cajoling. "There will be an inquiry, of course, but nothing is out there that cannot be explained away. I chair the oversight committee in the senate. Everything that we've done has been within the parameters of the committee guidelines. I promise you that."

Even from so far away, Noah could hear the lie in the words. Damon was leery as well.

"But what about the raid? Anton's assistant told me that he heard Anton being captured over an open cell line."

Senator Hall sighed. "Damon, you have to remember, those camps are in places that no one wants to be for a reason. It might have been a rebel uprising or a tribal attack. We have no way of knowing until someone goes down there and actually checks."

"I sent a man down there," Damon snapped, "and he hasn't reported in. And neither has any of his team."

Glass clinked like drinks were being poured. "I'll put out some feelers and see what the locals are talking about. I have a feeling it's something related to the government of the country. When things go dark like this, like through a coup, it takes a few days for basics to get back on line, like power and cell phones. Don't stress out until you absolutely need to."

There was the sound of muffled footsteps on carpet, like he was crossing the room. "Now, have a drink and relax. This is all going to work out the way it needs to. And when the research that Dr. Shu did comes to light, you and your company will be deemed heroes."

Again, the thread of mistruth in the words.

"Do you have my payment?"

There was some rustling again, then a clink of glass. This tone was different from the drinks glasses, though.

"That's all? I expected there to be more."

"These vials contain the most concentrated form of the drug. You have no idea of the process it takes to get just this. Use it wisely."

The senator huffed and moved behind his desk. "Oh, I will."

Their talk faded away, like they were walking outside, so Noah's attention shifted. He found true gold in a closet, he thought, in a secure wing on the north side of the house. It was a man and a woman's voices, and Noah could tell they were kissing, passionately.

"It's just for a little bit longer," a woman whispered. He thought it might be Victoria, Cameron Hall's wife.

"It has to change," the man snapped. "I don't know how much longer I can do this."

Noah recognized the timbre of his teammate's voice. Chris Taylor was a conniving ass on the best of days. Extra slimy on his worst. If Noah was on fire in the middle of the street, Chris Taylor wouldn't get out of his lawn chair to piss on him. Noah knew that for a fact.

"You can do it for as long as I tell you to do it, Taylor. We're almost in the clear."

"Are we really though? You keep saying that."

The woman sighed, though it was muffled. Noah cocked his head, trying to find a better acoustic point. The couple was deep in the mansion and their voices were the hardest to hear so far. Could he move closer?

He glanced back at the bedroom door. Blake was in there, playing on his iPad. The boy was Noah's highest priority. Glancing down the hallway, he decided he could walk down to that corner, but no further.

As soon as he did the voices came in clearer. The woman was wheedling; he could hear the pout in her words.

"I know how incredibly hard you've worked to do this. We are so close. Within hours, I think. Cameron is going to take care of Wilkes and the kid late tonight or early morning, he said, and by the time he realizes I've cleaned out the safe, we'll be long gone."

There was a masculine chuckle, and the distinctive sound of a zipper. Then there was rustling, and a long exhale. "You know, you can't always distract me with a blowjob."

"Hmm. I'm not. It's been weeks since I've seen you. I have needs, Taylor, and the old fucker downstairs can't get it up anymore."

Taylor chuckled, and groaned, marking Noah's retreat. Time to go.

Noah drew back into himself, his head positively throbbing. When he touched beneath his nose, there was just a bit of blood and he wiped it away. He sifted through the information he'd heard. Between the tensions between the guards and the subterfuge going on with both Cameron *and* Victoria Hall, this house was a tinderbox, about to go up. It sounded like they had plans to take out Damon and Blake and he wasn't down with that. Wilkes could rot in hell for all he cared, but Blake was a damn decent kid. There was no reason for him to die.

A plan began to form in his mind, but he needed more information. In a few hours he would come out and *listen*, and make a final plan.

———

Wulfe paced from one room to the next, restless as hell. They were at the culmination of everything they'd set out to do, and now he was forced to cool his heels. Aiden had managed to put all of the information together. Fontana had rescued the men. Now it was his turn to dismantle the company. That had always been the plan. For years the Dogs of War had railed against the Silverstone Collaborative and vowed to take all the fuckers down. It was one of the reasons why they'd taken the name.

Elizabeth assuming leadership of the company threw a hell of a wrench into those plans, and put Wulfe into a predicament. It took a huge leap of faith to believe that she was never a part of the corruption within Silverstone. She'd been right there with Damon at the head of the company. If she was to be believed, though, she'd allowed him to take over the marketing and expansion, while she'd stayed cocooned on the research side, oblivious to the world outside her laboratory.

Wulfe remembered how much she'd enjoyed school. It had been one of her few escapes from her family. Even when they'd met for their liaisons, there had been a few times when she'd gone on about something fascinating she'd learned, and her dreams of finding a cure for the most basic of diseases. One of their dates, he remembered, had been cancelled because she'd been studying for her last final exam before graduation. Elizabeth had a sincere love of medicine, he had no doubt about that, but could that love have been corrupted by research gained through dubious means?

Wandering back toward the den, he looked for her form, bent over her laptop, but she wasn't there. Then he spotted her sitting in the cushioned window seat, her feet propped up, looking out over the too-green grass. The sun was beginning to go down. There was a thoughtful look on her pale face.

"There is food in the kitchen. Can I get you something?"

She looked up with a start, and a bit of a blush. "Oh, I'll get something in a while. I'm not really hungry."

Wulfe leaned against the frame of the window. She started to move her feet so that he could sit down but he grabbed her toes, holding her still. Then, changing his mind, he lifted her feet up, sat down, and rested them in his lap. Without conscious thought he began massaging her toes, then working his way up to her arches.

Elizabeth moaned, her head leaning back against the window frame behind her. "You know, you are the only one that ever did that for me."

He grinned, loving that little detail. "I remember how much you enjoyed it. And how much it made you relax."

"Next you'll be rushing me into the bath," she said with a laugh, then she seemed to catch herself.

Yes, that was a very dangerous direction to go. Once it was put into the air, though, it seemed to echo and grow. When they'd been together, he'd been fascinated with everything about her. Learning that baths made her pliant and happy, he'd made sure to try to fit them into their time, if he could. More than once he'd joined her in the bath, and he could remember the carefree feeling of her love as he cradled her to him.

His body remembered— too clearly— and it began to respond beneath her feet.

Elizabeth looked at him, her eyes darkening as she sighed out a breath. "Oh, Wulfe. I miss those times, I'm not going to lie, but we have to be careful. There's so much going on right now." Her voice trailed off, but her feet shifted just the tiniest bit, as if she couldn't help herself.

Wulfe knew they were walking a dangerous line. She was married, with a child. There was a possibility she would be charged with atrocious crimes, her business ruined. In that moment, he didn't care about any of that. He wanted to feel the way she'd made him feel ten years ago, free and happy and content. It was one of the things he'd dreamed about when he'd been in the cage. Elizabeth. His Liz. He folded both of his hands over her foot and just held her there for a long moment, before letting her go.

Elizabeth folded her knees in front of her and wrapped her arms around them, her gaze drifting out the window. "I thought about you a lot after we separated. I want you to know," she paused, looking down. "I want you to know that I appreciated the man you were. You showed me how a man should treat a woman, and I needed that. I'd never experienced love before."

Her eyes lifted and he would have stabbed himself in the heart for her if it would have taken away her pain. Reaching out, he drew his fingers down the length of her satiny ponytail, wishing he dared draw her into his arms. He glanced at the door of the room. Standing wide open, of course. If Rose walked by right this moment, every scrap of information they'd struggled to eke out of the past two years could be compromised by the position they were in. *Scheisse*, the CIA probably had cameras all through this house.

Letting his hand fall to his lap, he sat back against the wood. "I experienced love like never before as well. It carried me through a lot of days, just remembering it." His voice roughened. This... *emotion* was hard to deal with.

Tears filled her eyes but she wiped them away. "This is such an impossible situation."

Yes, it most definitely was.

In an effort to make it easier on them both, he changed topic. "Has your research turned up anything new?"

She blinked, obviously shifting gears in her mind. "A few things. I've found a few password encrypted files in Damon's email. It's not his normal series of passwords, so it's going to take me a bit to figure them out. He always writes it down somewhere, I just have to find it. And I've found a few things about keeping info away from me." She gave him an ironic look. "I'm forwarding that info on to a Dropbox address Rose gave me. Hopefully it'll go on the Pro side of my board rather than the Con."

He shared her irony, giving her a smile. "It's the new favorite buzzword, *transparency*."

"Yes, but I'm okay with it." Her expression turned pensive. "There's been too much secrecy connected to the Silverstone Collaborative."

Wulfe agreed, and he appreciated that Elizabeth could see that. Now to see if she would put everything she was saying into motion.

"So," she murmured softly, "along those lines... can you tell me about your involvement?"

Wulfe blinked, hating that she'd asked but understanding her motivations. "I was in the German version of your own Navy SEALs when a man approached us, almost four and a half years ago now. I was told that I had an opportunity to be in a top secret, multinational research program only offered to the elite of military around the world. Of course, being the German I was, I had to try it. At first it was... challenging, then it got hard and the men began to rebel. There were several different nationalities there, but we all drew together to protest our treatment. We were in the jungles of Brazil, nothing around us but jungle and mosquitos. And Brazilian Army. One day they put us through training, we went to bed, and we woke up in cages, naked. They had drugged us. We were no longer allowed to leave, and they treated us as hostiles as they continued to test on us."

Elizabeth looked shocked, her heart racing. One hand covered her mouth.

"The 'training' got considerably harder when we became prisoners. They injected us with sicknesses and disease. Common things at first, then more dangerous ones. Many of the men died. In those first days Shu was developing the serum on site, from the plant itself. Sometimes the mixture was too strong and they inadvertently killed the prisoner. Other times the disease did. I lasted through it. And a few other men did, though it was a near thing. I had lost forty-two pounds. They had us on this special diet ration..."

His voice trailed off. Liz's face had lost all color and her eyes were glossy, like she was about to cry. Wulfe appreciated the emotion, but he didn't want her to suffer. He shrugged lightly, trying to play it off. "It was very nice eating an American burger on my brother's plane on the way home."

She shook her head. "No, tell me all of it. No more sugar-coating. You left out a large chunk."

He shifted on the bench, letting her feet go as he turned from the window. "I did leave out some," he admitted, "but I don't want you to hurt like I have."

"I appreciate that, Wulfe, but I can't make the decisions I need to if I don't have all of the information."

There was determination in her eyes now, and some of the color had returned to her cheeks. Yes, perhaps she did need it all. Planting his elbows on his knees, he sighed.

"As much as I hate to admit it, Shu was a bit of a genius. The Ayahuasca serum was refined and refined until even gunshot wounds could repair themselves, sometimes within hours. Broken bones knitted themselves, skin sealed over. But the most interesting aspect, which we didn't let the guards or doctors know about, was that our mental capacity seemed to expand, which is actually what the witch doctors used to for in the jungle. I'm not even sure who realized it first, but we started being able to talk to each other mind to mind— tele-pathically. *If* we were close enough together. Then we were able to influence the guards with a mental thought. We each developed these... abilities."

He spread his hands wide as he talked. "We haven't tested it a lot, but we all have abilities in different areas. Then Shu died from snakebite. We heard Mattingly was coming in to take over and we suspected that life would get much harder than it already was. We began to plan. We knew we weren't going to get any stronger on starvation rations and locked in those cages. So one night, Fontana kicked us in the ass and we left. We tried to gather as much food as we could, and we stole what information we could find. Then we set fire to the medical building as a distraction and headed into the jungle. It took us days, but we made it to the coast and I called Nikolas, my brother. He thought someone was pranking him, but within hours he was there. He flew us away just before the Bitch in Blue caught us."

"And you've been on the run since then."

"Yes," he said softly. "We each took some of the information we'd stolen to hide, and we built ourselves back up. My brother has been integral to regaining my health. He hid me for a long time while I recovered."

She blinked, turning to sit next to him. "He was always a decent guy, if I remember correctly."

"Yes," Wulfe agreed. He would do anything for Nikolas.

"The company eventually realized we had the information about the drug with us, but we never stayed still long enough to get caught with it. Fontana ran interference for us for a long time, planting distractions, pretending burglaries."

Her eyes widened and she leaned toward him. "Wait, the guy that's been rattling our security for the past two years is your buddy?"

Wulfe grinned. "Yes."

"I remember Damon bitching about him. He never really did much, just kept security running from one property to the next."

"Yes. In that time, though, your doctors here began to develop a drug comparable to Spartan. They would send operatives after us, or our families to test the drug. That was eventually what drew us out of hiding. They knew who we were as well as who our family was. Nikolas was almost kidnapped, and Aiden's pregnant sister-in-law almost killed when they went after his brother. It was time to connect again, get all of the information together and come for the company, as well as your husband and anyone else involved."

"My God..." she breathed. "This is so surreal. I mean, for the past five years I've been raising my son and working on several of my own projects. I never knew any of this was going on. Not until you told me to start digging. I feel so stupid. This is *my* company and I had blinders on the whole time," she said, anger threading her voice.

The entire time he'd been telling her the story, he'd been reading her emotions. She'd responded as anyone would being told the story for the first time, with fear and disbelief and concern. There had been no inappropriate surges of anything. Certainly no guilt. He believed her when she said she had no idea. And he believed her when she said she was going to change the company. In her heart and mind she believed it was going to happen.

Reaching out, she cupped his hand in her own. "I wish I had been there for you," she murmured.

Again, truth, and it was going to break his heart. "I'm going to go talk to Officer Rose about something."

This had been a heavy conversation. He needed a break.

CHAPTER SEVEN

Blake didn't know where Noah had gone. Maybe he'd gone to take a nap somewhere. No, that didn't seem right. Noah very rarely ever left him.

Blake was going crazy. There was nothing to do here. The senator had great WiFi, but even he got tired of the tablet eventually. He wanted to go see that dog again, the one that had smiled for him.

Yeah, he knew the big black German Shepherd was supposed to be scary, but Blake didn't feel like the dog liked his job. It had to be boring, walking the same circles over and over again. The senator had a decent sized piece of land considering where it was. This area had to be expensive. It reminded him of the neighborhood in the Hamptons where the Cole estate was. Stinking rich. Expensive cars everywhere. Cold servants.

Walking to the window, he looked down onto the grounds. There had to be a kennel or something around, right? A place for the guards to keep the dogs. Maybe he would go for a walk and see what he could find.

He scratched out a note to Noah, grabbed his tablet in

case he wanted to take pictures, and headed out. If he was quick, he could be back before dinner. Before Noah even noticed he was gone. There were enough guards around here to keep him safe if anything happened.

Guilt twisted his belly. Noah hadn't exactly said he had to stay here, but it was kind of one of those understood things. Blake knew he was supposed to stay out of sight, but he was sooooo bored.

Twisting the handle on the French doors he let himself out of the room. He walked across the stone patio then jogged down the circular staircase on the side of the house. The big monster pool was back here and he assumed the other maintenance stuff would be back here too. It felt too open to cross by the pool so he circled around behind the pool house. As he did, voices drifted on the wind and he paused.

"It's too early," a woman hissed. "You know he's going to be watching it like a hawk."

"When Damon's at dinner might be a good time for you to sneak in there and look for it. It's a black case, almost looks like a wallet."

"When am I supposed to do that?" The woman's voice rose. "I have to be hostess with the mostess. You know Cameron will want me there."

The man sighed, and Blake thought he sounded familiar. Creeping up to the window, he glanced inside, but the curtains were blowing. The pool house was open on the front, but there was no way he was gonna go look. For just a second, the sheers blew apart and he could see Taylor, Dad's guard, and Mrs. Hall standing together.

Huh. That was weird. Then Taylor reached out and put his hand on Mrs. Hall's face.

"I just wanted you to know what was going on. I need to find Damon. I'm supposed to be on duty now so I'm going to go." Leaning forward he pressed a kiss to Mrs. Hall's lips.

Blake jerked back, his mouth falling open. A crazy giggle wanted to get out and he slapped a hand over his mouth to keep it in, then leaned in to look again.

"Don't worry, baby," Taylor whispered, before walking away.

Blake leaned up against the side of the pool house until Taylor's footsteps faded away.

"Hey," Mrs. Hall said, and Blake freaked. He whirled to the window, and it took him a second to realize that she was talking to someone on a cell phone.

"No, not yet. Should be tonight or early tomorrow morning. Are you sure audio will be enough?"

Frowning, he looked in through the window, but the curtains were still, blocking his view.

"Fine," she said eventually. "But you'd better be ready to grab my ass at a moment's notice. Do you understand?"

The other person must have answered correctly because she hung up, without even a goodbye. Blake moved close against the wall again, hiding behind a poofy frond thing. Mrs. Hall stalked out of the pool house and along the side of the pool, her high heels clicking all the way to the end. She stopped for a minute and seemed to be giving herself some kind of pep talk, then she walked up the steps and into the house.

Blake had just let out a breath when a heavy hand landed on his shoulder. Another went around his mouth. Fear jolting through him, he rolled his eyes to see who had him.

"Jeez, Noah, you scared the crap out of me!" He gasped as soon as the big hand was removed.

Noah flashed him the slightest of grins, then his face turned critical. "I know you were in your room when I left."

"Dude, I'm *bored*. Like, my brain is rotting out of my head bored. I needed to get out and do something. I thought I'd see if I could find that dog again."

Noah stared at him for a long moment before giving a slight nod. "Wrong direction, then."

Blake followed Noah as he wove through the foliage at the back of the pool. On the far side there was a paved path down to a boat dock. Blake had seen the senator's boat. It was huge. When you were on it you couldn't even feel the motion of the water underneath. What was it called? Bill Pusher or something like that. One of those things that adults say is "so clever" but doesn't make sense.

Noah led him along a small path to the right. It was landscaped with pretty thick bushes so you didn't even realize it was there until you pushed some fronds out of the way. They hiked down the path for about fifty feet, then they came to a clearing. There were two small barns. The one on the right looked to be for maintenance, because there were a bunch of bags of mulch sitting out front, and rakes leaning against the front of the barn. The second barn, on the left, had been made into a kennel. As soon as they stepped into the clearing, the dog in the outside run started barking his fool head off. Noah circled the cages and there on the other side was the dog that Blake had met earlier in the day.

Seben stood at attention but seemed to recognize Blake. Inching to the cage, Blake knelt on the ground outside the fence and held his hand out.

"Slowly," Noah told him.

Yeah, he knew. Blake loved dogs and loved to pet them. He always asked if it was okay to say hi to a dog and pet them. Dogs really liked him. Even Mrs. Chang's nasty terrier mix that lived in the townhouse next to theirs in the city seemed to like him, and he usually bit everyone else. Mom had promised that they would get a dog *someday*, but it just wasn't convenient when they lived in the city so much. He went to school most of the day and she worked a lot. They had servants, but *he* wanted to have the dog and take care of it. Not give it to the servants.

As he looked at Seben, he decided that this was the kind of dog he wanted. Actually, he wanted Seben. The dog neared the fence and Blake reached his hand through to stroke his soft, black muzzle. The dog in the cage beside them finally quieted down and seemed curious about what was going on.

Blake caught sight of the tag hanging from the collar. "What does Seben mean, Noah?"

"It means Seven in German."

Blake nodded. "That makes sense. This breed started in Germany." Then something occurred to him. "Wait. Do you think they named him that because he didn't get a regular name?"

Curiously, he looked at the dog in the cage beside Seben's. Talking softly, he drew close enough to the second dog, a Belgian Malinois, to look at the same silver tag.

"Sech-es," he sounded out.

"Sechs," Noah said easily, but the ways he said it sounded like Zeks. "It means six."

Blake drew back and looked at the dogs, his heart sad. "Six and seven. They didn't even bother to give them names."

"They're working dogs. They were bought and trained for a job."

Blake looked up at Noah. The man was calm and controlled, but Blake could hear the tiniest bit of anger in his voice. He didn't agree with the way the dogs were treated either.

What could he actually do about it though?

Seben leaned against the fence. Blake reached through and rubbed him all over, trying to give him some companionship or love or whatever he needed. Seben's long plume of a tail wagged happily the whole time. The dog was beautiful, but he was stuck here in a cage all his life. The dog was wearing a second collar and Blake explored it with his fingers. Through the fur he could feel callused patches of skin. "What is this?"

"It's a shock collar," Noah said slowly. "If the dog misbehaves he can be punished by the handler."

Blake scowled. Without hesitation he unbuckled the nasty thing, drew it through the chain link fence and threw it away into the brush. "No one should live like that, afraid to move when they do what comes naturally."

He looked at Noah, expecting to be scolded, but Noah gave him a grim smile. "You're exactly right, Blake."

He moved to Sechs' cage and reaching through carefully, unfastened the collar and threw it into the brush. He stroked the dog's ears, then moved back to Seben's cage. For some reason this dog really appealed to him, and he didn't understand why. "I wish..."

It wasn't worth even saying. With the way things were going in his life he had a feeling he would never get a dog. Unfolding the case from his tablet he took a couple of pictures of the dogs.

"Let's get back to the house buddy. You'll probably have to go down for dinner soon."

Blake sighed. "Can I tell them I'm sick or something? I don't want to go down there and they don't want me there. I'd much rather eat in my room with you."

He asked all the time and Noah usually said no, but today, his lips tightening, he gave a single nod. "I'll ask your dad when we get back up there."

Blake tried not to get too excited because he'd probably be disappointed, but he appreciated that Noah would try. Looking way, way up to the man, he held a fist out. They bumped knuckles and grinned at each other.

They turned toward the path and Noah stopped suddenly,

stepping directly in front of Blake. Blake went still, his training kicking in. Noah had taught him that if there was ever trouble, he would take the danger, whatever it was. He was supposed to stand directly behind Noah, hand on his belt, until they figured out what was going on, then he was to listen to Noah's orders precisely. They'd done drills. Every once in a while Noah would step in front of him on the street, and Blake would go still like a deer, grabbing the back of Noah's belt. Sometimes people looked at them weird, but he kind of enjoyed having that secret communication with Noah.

Now, though, something made his heart race.

"Listen to me, asshole," some man snarled. "Stay away from the dogs."

Both of Noah's hands went out from his body, palm up. "We didn't mean any harm. The boy was just curious."

"I don't care if he was, it's a restricted area back here."

Blake peered around the edge of Noah's body. A short guy with dark hair and mean eyes stood about ten feet away. He stomped to the cages and banged on the fence with some kind of rod thing. Both dogs launched into a flurry of aggressive barking and Blake thought the guy would be in trouble if the dogs ever got out of the cages.

Noah cupped his shoulder and moved him down the path. They'd rounded the bend when they heard the man curse behind them. "Where the hell are the collars?!"

They set off in a jog, Noah bringing up the rear to protect Blake. Blake had always thought it was a little much, protecting him like that, but he appreciated it.

"Let's get back to the room, Hoss."

———

Damon watched Cameron's wife's face, but he wasn't really

listening to her. Victoria Hall was the typical privileged blonde less than half the age of her current husband, the senator. She pranced around in her mini-skirt and heels like she was auditioning for the next Housewives reality series. She looked nice, but she definitely wasn't his type.

Looked too much like Elizabeth.

So he was curious why she was up here yammering at him.

"That's great," he cut her off. "I'll tell Elizabeth the next time I see her. If you don't mind I'm going to go relax for a bit."

She smiled at him like he'd said something funny, but he was done with her. Turning his back, he walked away from her, toward the bedroom.

Taylor, his guard, was standing at the door to his bedroom. The man looked strong and healthy, exactly like the former Marine he was. Damon knew he was curious about why they were there at the senator's house, but he didn't feel like indulging the man's curiosity. As good a guard as he was, he was imbecilic when it came to politics and strategy. Taylor probably thought he didn't know about the affair he was carrying on with the Senator's wife. The pretty ones were not always the brightest.

"Go get yourself some dinner, Taylor. I'm going to take a nap before dinner."

"Yes, sir."

Letting himself into the room, he closed the door in Taylor's face. Crossing to the armoire, he opened the door. The maids were efficient in this house and the few things he'd packed had been pressed and hung. He didn't see the black case... his heart began to race as he sifted through his things.

Crossing to the bathroom, he looked at the vanity. Yes, there it was. Unzipping it he looked at the two vials of amber liquid. The third he'd just handed over to Cameron as payment for the support he'd given him over the past couple years. It was the final payment after several long years of kissing ass. These vials were the culmination of the Marathon Program, the follow up to the Spartan Project. When the good Dr. Shu had died unexpectedly and the information on how to create Spartan had disappeared, they'd had to work with the little bit of information they had on hand at the Arlington facility. The serum they'd come up with didn't have the efficacy of the Spartan serum, or the drama of the Leonidas serum, but it was the best they had. Leonidas had worked remarkably well on Priscilla, but she had been the aberration. They'd tried it on fifteen Silverstone volunteers, mostly security guards, with no results. It had eventually been scrapped. Marathon still had too many bugs, but it actually had a more effective rate on the subjects, and it was going to have to do. It was the only collateral he had to get out of the country alive.

Though the power it created wasn't as flashy as the other serums, Marathon was a more broad-use enhancer.

When Priscilla had been killed—as bullet-proof as she was, both literally and figuratively—he'd known that things were unraveling, and he needed to be ready to get out of Dodge. The pot was boiling over, so to speak, and he needed to get out of the country before it burned him up. The company was a lost cause. It was going to be locked up in federal charges for years, and would end up going under, more than likely. Yes, he'd probably be charged as well, but if he worked it right with the French official he'd been courting, there would be no extradition back to the U.S. to face those charges.

The town he'd picked out in France was a lovely community and with what he was about to earn, he'd be able to support a *very* comfortable lifestyle.

It wasn't like he had anything left here.

His marriage was a joke. He should have signed the

divorce paperwork months ago, but he'd been holding out for more money. Now he doubted he'd ever see any of it, because it would take too long for the divorce to be finalized. He would just have to get the money out of the ice queen in other ways.

Grinning, he zipped up the case and stowed it inside one of the vanity drawers, in the very back corner. He wasn't sure how long he would be staying here. Probably only a few days. Cameron didn't appreciate being complicit in a kidnapping.

On impulse, Damon pulled the case out again. He'd already left it unsupervised once. He didn't want to do that again. Where could he hide it? Glancing around the room, nothing seemed appropriate. It all seemed too obvious. Where would they *not* look?

And maybe he should split up the vials. If one was found he would still have a second. Slipping one glass tube from beneath the elastic he looked for a place to put it, but nothing seemed appropriate. Grabbing one of the beige wash cloths he rolled a vial up in it, then stuck it in his accessory bag. A little bulky, but it would probably escape notice. Now, what to do with the second? It should be away from his person.

Tucking the case into the waistband of his pants in case he encountered anyone, he left the room and headed down the empty hallway. This wing was devoted to guests and they always stayed in the same rooms. Blake's room was two doors down from his own. Noah was nowhere to be seen. Letting himself into the room, he looked around. No Blake or Noah.

His gaze caught on the bedraggled black backpack on the bed. Blake had carried the same bag for two years now, and he very rarely left it anywhere. It was open, like Blake had grabbed something out of it before taking off. Crossing the room, Damon searched the contents. Miscellaneous junk that a nine year old would think was important. It also appeared to be stuff that he'd put in and forgotten about. There were a few school papers from months ago. Arguing with himself internally, he debated leaving the black case in the bag. He doubted Blake would ever find it and really, who would think to search a kid? They'd be together for the foreseeable future.

Elizabeth's texts had gotten increasingly frantic. At some point he would have to respond to her, but he'd let her burn for another day or so. It was hard for him to evoke any emotion in her, but he knew her soft spot. Blake. In a few days, after he'd let her stew long enough, she'd be willing to hand over the moon to get her son back.

The kid was great—wildly intelligent, compassionate, caring. Damon had raised him with as much attention and care as his own frigid parents had taken with his upbringing. For a moment, his conscience pricked at him. It wasn't the kid's fault that his father was an asshole. He had raised Blake as he'd been raised, at arm's length. The only hitch in that plan was Elizabeth. Though their marriage had been nothing more than a cold contract, he had to admit that she'd been a wonderful mother to his son. She'd lavished so much love and attention on the boy that Damon had wondered what that felt like at times. If he'd been the focus of the tiniest bit of that care, maybe things would have turned out differently between them. It never occurred to him that had he shown her the slightest bit of attention or affection, things might have been different as well. But he'd never been interested in Elizabeth's emotions or feelings, just her family's company.

There was a meeting scheduled in two days in Miami. Delegates from seven countries would be there and one vial of Marathon would be sold to the highest bidder. The third vial would be going with him to France, to be used at his discretion. It would probably be 'payment' to the French government for helping him deal with what was going on now. Once the Miami meeting was concluded, they would all be going their separate ways. Then he could focus on milking Elizabeth for all of the family money he could.

Tucking the case into the very bottom of the backpack, he shoved all the other shit on top of it. Then he left the pack in the same position he'd found it in and walked out the door.

CHAPTER EIGHT

When her cell phone pinged with an incoming message, Elizabeth rushed across the bedroom to grab it. She entered the code wrong the first time and had to redo it because her hands were shaking.

It was a new email from Blake.

Hey, mom. just got back from the kennel they keep the guard dogs in. The one I like is called Seben and that means seven in German. Don't be mad but I stole a collar off of him and threw it away. It was a shock collar and there were spots on his neck where his trainer burned him. That made me mad.

Dad has some kind of business deal going on with the senator and we're kind stuck here for a couple of days. I'm bored and I wish you were here. Why didn't you come with us?

Here's another picture of the dog I like. Can we get one like him?

Love you.

There was another dog picture attached, this one taken through a chain link fence and a little out of focus. She smiled because Blake had taken a picture of his own hand petting the dog.

Sinking to the bed, Elizabeth let the relief roll over her

like a wave. Blake was fine. They knew exactly where he was and what he was doing. In the interest of her new transparency rule, she left the room she'd been assigned and headed down the hallway to the office where Rose had set himself up. Wulfe and two other men were inside, but she crossed to the desk where Rose sat. Swiping the phone on again, she held it out for him to read the email.

"Business deal, huh?" Rose murmured. "Any idea what he means?"

She shook her head, crossing her arms and holding her elbows. "I have no idea. I know he's worked with the senator before, but I don't know what he's down there for specifically. I know the company has worked with him several times. Even I've talked to him about what was expected out of a certain drug. Nothing compromising, of course, just minor chit chat over dinner."

Rose nodded, scrolling through her emails a little. Elizabeth bristled but decided it didn't really matter. He probably had access to every email and social media account she had already now that she was officially cooperating with them.

She looked at Wulfe, standing over by the window. He was frowning, and seemed to understand her building desperation. "If we don't move soon," he said, "there's a chance he could take the boy out of the country. Once he's outside our borders it becomes much harder to find him."

Officer Rose flicked a glance at Wulfe.

"I understand that, but if we can get more evidence, especially on the senator, we need to try. He's been under investigation for years, and this could be what finally puts him over the edge." He ran his hand through his dark hair, looking aggravated. "What you don't understand, Mrs. Wilkes, is that I'm under orders as well. And I will run this operation to maximize the charges I can get. Believe it or not, kidnapping your son is one of the more minor charges against him."

Elizabeth could appreciate the determination she could see in the officer's expression and his steady brown eyes, but this was her son's safety they were talking about. Her anger began to build and she took the phone from his hand. "Mr. Rose, let me be perfectly frank. You have," she glanced at her watch, "four hours to decide what you're going to do, or I'm going to get a car, drive over there and walk away from the property with my son. The house staff knows me and if Cameron Hall is trying to keep this whole big sordid mess quiet, he won't have told his staff anything of his plans. They definitely will have no idea that Damon is threatening the welfare of my child. They will hand my son over to me without hesitation."

Rose stared at her for a long moment, and she couldn't read much of what he was thinking. "Then your soon-to-be ex will have nothing keeping him in the States. Even though we haven't heard anything out of him, I believe Damon is going to try to leverage your son for money. He's involved in some kind of business deal right now, but as soon as it's complete you're going to be hearing from Damon, I guarantee."

Yes, that was what she'd been thinking too.

"And as soon as Damon gets money out of you," Rose continued, "he's going to run, and we will get no satisfaction for the men he tortured and killed."

Elizabeth hated this situation. She wanted for all those men to be vindicated, of course, but her son was her primary focus. He always had been. "My statement stands," she said softly, and left the office.

Wulfe watched her go, admiring the spirit. It wasn't easy to stand up to the CIA, but she'd done it. Years ago she wouldn't have been able to do it, but maturity and experience had given her assurance.

Rose was scowling, and the frustration rolling off of him

was substantial. His hands were tied and he didn't like being given ultimatums, but what did the man expect? This safe house was less than three miles, literally just streets away, from her son. Wulfe thought Elizabeth was being remarkably patient. If his child was so close there would be no stopping him. He would retrieve the boy at all costs.

Wulfe glanced at his watch. It was just past seven o'clock in the evening. Maybe once everyone had settled in for the night, he would slide out and go for a walk.

———

Noah felt on edge. They'd just come back from dinner and things had been more tense than normal. Senator Cameron Hall and his wife had sat at one end of the table, and Damon and Blake had sat at the other. Security stood off to the side or in another room entirely. Noah preferred to stand outside the dining room entrance, on the kitchen side. It gave him a good vantage point from every direction, and put him closest to Blake.

Noah had been on the Silverstone Collaborative security teams for a couple of years now and this was his preferred assignment, watching the boy. Now, if an armed gunman came in and began spraying the room, Noah would try to get Damon and Blake out, but as of this second, Blake was his main priority.

So, when Blake innocently asked where his mother was, and Damon snapped, "Who the fuck cares," he found himself at cross-purposes. Blake's face immediately clouded with angry tears and Noah had the almost overwhelming impulse to go in and beat the ever-loving fuck out of Damon Wilkes.

Victoria Hall giggled into the silence, and Noah could have put a bullet in her head at that moment as well. Blake's face reddened even more, and Noah could feel the anger and frustration seething inside him. It practically radiated off of him.

When Blake stood and made his excuses to Senator Hall, Noah though his heart would burst with pride as the boy left the room with his chin up. Noah left his post and followed on Blake's heels and as soon as they cleared the doorway, he rested a hand on his shoulder. Blake kept his emotions under wraps, though.

As they climbed the stairway toward the bedrooms, Noah could hear the senator admonish Damon Wilkes. He paused and motioned Blake on ahead.

"You're about to scar that boy for the rest of his life, have you thought about that Damon? I haven't said anything, but the way you're going about this is cruel."

Damon laughed. "You think, huh? Good. Elizabeth can deal with the little bastard. I'm so done with it all."

"Damon," the senator said soothingly, "In a few more hours this will all be over and you will be winging your way to France. Don't lose your cool now."

Noah wondered if Damon heard the thread of lie in the senator's voice.

"I'm not losing my cool," Damon growled. "I'm just pissed. She's dismissing me from the company like a damn intern. This deal has to work or I'm fucked."

Noah heard a chair scrape back and the sound of foot-steps retreating from the room as Damon left, then a heavy sigh from the senator.

"He is not in the mood to be teased," Victoria said. "Do you think he was in love with his security woman, like people have been saying?"

"I don't know. He needs a thicker skin, and he's not going to grow it in the next day or two," Cameron murmured. His voice sounded resigned, like he'd come to some decision.

"What are you going to do, Cam?" Victoria asked quietly.

"I'm not going to lie, he puts me on edge. I don't dig into your business dealings, but I know you've taken care of our future before. If he's kidnapped that boy, and our names are brought into it for housing him..." she let her voice trail off.

"Don't worry about it, dear heart. I'll take care of everything. I have a plan in the works and it will all be over with by morning. Just stay in your room tonight."

There were clicking sounds like they were kissing.

"I'm going to go unwind in the bath. Feel free to join me," she murmured.

"You go ahead, dear. I have a lot to do right now."

Noah drew back, anxiety building in his gut. Something was definitely going to happen tonight and he didn't want Blake to be anywhere near it. It was time to go.

He scanned the area, looking for security as he and Blake climbed the stairs. The senator's men stayed on the exterior of the house for the most part, but Damon's were still inside. There was a servants' area in the back of the house, and they'd been staying there. Damon didn't have plans to move until tomorrow night, so they were technically off-shift. They wouldn't be a problem.

The senator's men, on the other hand, could be an issue. He would have to listen like he never had before.

When he entered the bedroom, Blake was standing at the bedroom window, arms crossed over his narrow chest. Crossing to him, Noah wondered what he could say to the nine year old to make him feel better about what had happened. He'd been flat out humiliated.

"They had no right to do that to you. Especially your dad."

Those narrow shoulders shrugged. "He never really liked me much, and I think he and Mom only stayed together for me." He glanced up at Noah. "I think he loved Ms. Mattingly.

And when she died he kind of did, too. He hasn't been the same since then."

Noah sighed and cocked a leg out. "Between you and me and the wall there? Yeah. I think he and Ms. Mattingly had something going on."

Blake nodded like he'd already known the answer.

The silence lengthened, but it didn't feel as painful as before. "Why don't you pack your bag, Hoss?"

Blake looked up at him in surprise. "What? Why?"

"I'm gonna take you back to your mom, but it's gotta be a secret. We can't tell anyone you're leaving, okay?"

The boy nodded, wide-eyed. "You're really going to take me back?"

Noah nodded and spread his arms as the boy lunged at him. He patted his back and squeezed him before letting him go. "We'll get out of here after dark, okay?"

He had no idea when the senator would be implementing his plan, but he hoped it would be later in the night when everyone should be in bed. There was a narrow window of safety he was playing with and he prayed his instincts would lead him right.

CHAPTER NINE

Wulfe heard Elizabeth's door open and grinned. He'd underestimated her. When she'd told Rose four hours, he'd expected her to wait out the time, but she was impressing him. Stretching out his senses, he tried to locate the other officers in the house. Four were in bedrooms, two were smoking outside and the other three were in the kitchen. Moving soundlessly, he left his own bedroom and paced down the hallway behind her. Reaching the corner as she began to head down the steps, he let out a breath of a hiss.

Elizabeth jerked, her pale eyes wide in her face. He would have laughed at the guilt written on her expression, but he didn't want anyone to hear. "This way," he mouthed.

There was a fire escape accessible from his window. He'd almost laughed when he'd seen it. A ladder to a window didn't seem like a very secure safe house. He'd looked it over and even reached out to touch the metal, but there didn't seem to be any sensors on it. Presumably there were cameras on the exterior the officers would monitor, perhaps from the kitchen where they were grouped.

Lifting the sash, Wulfe motioned Elizabeth closer and leaned down to whisper into her ear. "This is probably on camera, so we're going to go down as fast as possible and with as little noise as possible. *Verstehen sie?*"

She nodded, eyes huge in her pale face. He gave her a motion and she went through the window. He moved directly behind her, trying to muffle their noises as much as possible with his abilities. If it had been raining it would have been a lot easier. Florida was known for pop-up thunderstorms, but it had been dry since they'd been here. And hot.

They reached the bottom and he grabbed her hand, taking the lead. She wore dark clothing and had a small leather backpack, which he assumed had all her essentials. She'd taken the time to plan her move carefully. Skirting the edges of the shadows, he paused at the rear corner of the house. There were two small cameras set above them, angled to catch as much of the yard as possible. Wulfe looked up at the cameras and concentrated.

Fontana was best with the electronic manipulation, but Wulfe could handle his fair share, especially when he was touching the object, like he was now. He *felt* the cameras fuzz out, and he jerked Elizabeth into a run. She kept up with him well, her long runner's legs stretching to keep up with his. When they reached a fence, he cupped his hands and boosted her up to the top. Then, leaping for all he was worth, he gained the top as well and dropped to the opposite side. Then he held his arms out for Elizabeth.

Without hesitation she dropped down, allowing him to catch her. Grinning, Wulfe dropped a quick kiss to her lips. "Well, done, *meine liebe*. Are you okay?"

She nodded, looking dazed but excited. "Yes."

"Let's go get your son."

———

Blake held his tablet out to Noah. "Mom's coming for me," he grinned.

Noah scanned the note. Excellent. "Tell her not to come here. I repeat. *Not here.* We'll meet her at the gates of the public marina north of here."

Blake nodded and tapped the message into his email, then sent it. Then he shoved the tablet into his bag and zipped it.

Noah was glad he'd caught that slight ping, otherwise they would have missed the message.

It was time to go. Tension was building in the house and he realized it was completely silent outside. He listened to his instincts. Stowing his earbuds because he would need every ounce of ability he had, he *listened* to the house and grounds. It was quiet for several long moments, then there was rustling and movement in the back, and a couple of sharp sounds. Those had almost sounded like silenced weapons, but he was so far away he couldn't be sure.

"Are you ready?" he whispered.

Blake nodded, his eyes huge in his face. He adjusted his hands around the straps of the backpack and clicked the sternum strap in place across his chest. "I'm ready, Noah."

"You do exactly as I say. Do you understand? Remember the hand motions?"

He went through a few of the motions and Blake stated what they meant.

Noah heard two more shots. Were those his own team-mates being taken out? There was a spate of *un*silenced gunfire, and Noah knew that was his team responding. They wouldn't just roll over and die. Using the distraction of their resistance, he would get the boy out.

Peering through the French doors, he looked for move-ment, but didn't see anything. Letting themselves out of the room, they crept along the patio and to the steps running down the side of the house. Blake kept one hand on Noah's back, just as he'd been instructed.

Noah stayed low, trying to minimize the size of the target, but he was a big guy. And they had a lot of yard to cross.

A dog began to bark at the far end of the house and Blake's attention turned that way. "That was Sechs," he said. "I recognize his bark."

There was a scream, like someone had been bitten, a gunshot then the whine of a dog. Noah knew the animal had been taken out, and so did Blake. The boy's eyes widened in the darkness and his mouth fell open. Noah thought he saw tears glimmering in the diffused light, but he didn't let him break down there. "We have to go."

They took off running. Noah guided them directly out from the North side of the house, then he began to swing west. If he could get them to the water, there were jet skis and boats and a half dozen other things he could use to get away.

Another dog barked and men began to shout. Had they been seen? Not daring to pause, he tightened his grip on Blake's wrist and ran even faster. He'd given up on stealth and was relying only on speed now, dragging the boy along.

Ahead of them was the tree line, and the paved path winding through the back of the property. A guard stepped out of the bushes to Noah's left, gun raised. Noah skidded to a stop and shoved Blake behind him.

Some of the men that had been treated with the Marathon drug had the ability to use mind control. Noah didn't, but he had developed a sub-sonic buzz that seemed to confuse and muddle thinking. He focused all of his energy on the guard, a man he'd met earlier in the day, and the man's hand began to waver. A frown twisted his face and he looked down at the gun in his hand. That slight distraction was enough for Noah to move forward and plow a meaty fist into the man's face. He went down like a ton of bricks.

There was a gasp behind him and he spun. Chris Taylor, his fellow teammate, held Blake in a chokehold. "Where the fuck are you going, Noah? Did you actually think you were going to slide out of here without anyone noticing?"

Noah held his hands up, not sure how to play the situation out. He had no respect for Taylor, and Taylor knew that. It was completely mutual.

"I'm doing what I'm paid to do; protecting the boy. Let go of him, Taylor."

Taylor only grinned. "I don't know. Seems to me like we might need a bargaining chip to get out of here. Have you noticed the Senator's guards have turned on us?"

"Yes," he growled, wanting to lunge forward and snatch Blake out of his grip. "Where's Wilkes?"

Taylor shrugged. "I wasn't on him when they came in the house. I have no idea where he is."

Noah scowled. Taylor had no business being a personal protection guard. He had no loyalty other than to his own skin.

"Think your mistress was behind this?"

Taylor's head jerked back in surprise and he laughed. "Oh, Noah, you have been busy. No, I don't think she's behind this, but I'm sure she'll take advantage of the situation."

There was the sound of feet running on the pavers around the pool, and they looked that way. Four men were running in their direction, guns drawn.

"We need to get out of here, Taylor," he hissed.

There was a moment of indecision on Taylor's face, then he motioned Noah ahead of him and shoved Blake toward him. Noah was more than happy with that and snatched the boy up into his arms. If Taylor wanted to be their meat shield he would totally let him. He pelted down the path toward the dock. Guns were firing haphazardly behind him. Marathon had given Taylor the fascinating ability to blur his form. So at night, with chaos reigning and bullets flying, he had a very good chance of making it out alive.

Noah felt something slam into his shoulder, but he kept his feet. Blake cried out. Had it hit him as well? He didn't have time to stop to check.

The senator's boat slip only held the big yacht, but there was a personal speedboat at the next property that Noah had scoped out when he'd done his initial security check. There was a gate and almost an acre of grass between he and his destination, though, and a hidden path through trees meant to provide privacy. Branches smacked at his face as he ran along the path. He tried to protect Blake's body, but he was more concerned with speed.

There was a sound behind them that sounded like a body going down. Noah glanced behind long enough to see Taylor crash to the deck, and one of the senator's guards leap over his body. Noah thought it had been the dog handler they'd pissed off earlier in the day. Taylor had apparently taken out three of the guards, which was impressive. Noah swung back. There was a gate thirty feet in front of him he had to get over. In front of him, wood shattered, exactly where he planned to go over. *Fuck!*

Noah slowed to a stop and turned, setting Blake to the ground and pushing him behind him.

The guard grinned, realizing that Noah had stopped. "This is going to be a pleasure."

Though he was too far away, Noah tried to focus on the guard's mind. Using every bit of his mental strength, until blood dripped from his nose, he stared at the aggressor, projecting pain. The man paused, shook his head and seemed to waver. The pause was just long enough for Seben to race in from the dark and clamp down on his arm.

The gun went off but the bullet disappeared into the night. Noah lunged toward the fight, but Seben had the guard sprawled on the ground by the time he got there. With a hammer punch to the man's jaw, Noah knocked him out. Seben, grinning with his very sharp teeth shining in the night, jogged over to Blake and lowered himself to the ground. Blake just stared at him for a long moment, and the dog seemed to deflate. Noah had never seen anything like it.

Then Blake grinned and reached out to pet the dog and everything was good. They still needed to get to the boat.

"We have to take him with us now."

There was no way Noah was going to say no to the boy, that dog had just saved his life.

Watching Seben warily, Noah took Blake's hand in his own and led him toward the access gate he could see crossing the path. He boosted Blake up over the wood and turned to the dog. Taking a chance, he motioned at the fence. "Over, Seben."

Without hesitation, the dog took a running leap and cleared the six-foot fence. Noah had never seen anything like it. Stepping back a bit, he took his own running leap. And fell right back to the ground when his left arm refused to work. *Shit!* His adrenalin had been running so hard he hadn't even felt the pain.

Walking off the trail he found a place where he could get a leg braced between a palm tree and the fence and he made it over. Before he dropped to the ground he looked back at the senator's estate. No movement.

Their luck held as they jogged down the dock at the next property. The key was in the ignition of the boat he'd picked out and it growled to life with a throaty purr. Blake and Seben hunkered down as out of sight as best they could. Noah unwound the tethers and pulled away from the dock, slowly at first, then picking up speed as he passed marker buoys. Turning right, he headed north toward the public marina.

CHAPTER TEN

Damon pushed off from the wall and jogged along the hallway, the shaving kit stuffed awkwardly in the waistband of his pants. It wasn't comfortable but it would have to do. He hadn't had time to grab his satchel. Gunshots echoed from outside and he wondered how the hell he was going to get out of this. This ... *aggression* was not his cup of tea. Priscilla had warned him that the people he was dealing with were very dangerous, but he'd never expected the senator to turn on him. There was a chance it was a hostile force invading the senator's house, but he seriously doubted that.

It was humiliating, but he hid in a supply closet for a while, until the gunfire had stopped. Several times he heard voices in the hallway and his heart would race, thinking they'd found him, but they would eventually pass on. He wondered if they would shoot Blake, a kid. The thought made him frown, some slight emotion twisting his stomach, but it wasn't enough to get him out of the closet. Blake had a guard. He'd be fine. He wondered where the fuck Taylor was. Probably with Victoria, laughing at the situation.

One thought pushed to the front of his brain. Get the second vial.

Pushing through into Blake's bedroom, he looked around. The boy was gone. His guard was gone. The bathroom was empty as well.

And there was no black backpack in sight.

Clenching his fists in fury, Damon wanted to scream out at the world, stupid *fate* that was forever interfering in his grand plans. Then he had to berate himself. Why the fuck had he put two pieces of collateral together? Quaking with anger, he looked around the room, trying to decide what to do. The meeting to sell the drug was tomorrow afternoon. If he could make it out of the senator's mansion in one piece, he knew exactly where the guard and Noah would go. Right back to the fucking ice queen— *Elizabeth*.

The French doors were standing open. Slipping through, he looked around, then jerked back into the shadows. Cameron Hall stood on the back patio, hands on hips, surveying the carnage. There were several bodies out here, of his own guards and Cameron's. Two of Cameron's guards stood in front of him, bleeding.

"Did you get the drug?" The state senator demanded, confirming Damon's suspicions.

The men shared a look. "Sir, we checked Mr. Wilkes' room for the case you described, but it's not in there. We also checked the boy's room and everywhere they might have been. The men chasing the boy and his guard haven't returned, so we have to assume they got away."

Cameron Hall was very good at masking his fury, but with his head tipped down, Damon could see it. "As soon as they make it to the authorities, they are going to tell them where they've been and who they've seen, and we're going to be in a serious political storm. Call Agent McCullough with the

Secret Service and have a clean-up crew sent out. We have to get a lid on this and try to minimize the damage."

"Yes, sir."

Damon's mind reeled. Everything was fucked up so badly... on an *epic* scale. *Fuck*. Wait, think, breathe. Well, he couldn't stay here. Maybe he could even get this mess to work for him.

Sidling along the building, he found a spiral staircase leading down to the pool deck. He didn't want Cameron to see him, but he needed to get out of here. Tiptoeing down the steps, feeling like a criminal, he tried to plan his escape, but there was no way he could. All he had his wallet, a shaving kit stuffed down his pants, and his phone, and no more than the clothes on his back, literally, because there was no way he was going back for his bag. He had no guards. Fucking Taylor had disappeared before the melee started, and he'd been the only enhanced soldier he'd had. All of the others had been with Truckle and Scofield in Guyana, presumably all dead now.

His pantheon, and all of the plans he had for it, had crumbled.

For the first time in years, all of the time he spent in the gym came in handy as he wove his way through the trees and bushes dotting Cameron's estate. Since all of the massacre was in the back, he headed toward the front of the house and angled out. Without his guards, he had no idea where he was, but he kept moving forward.

Then a figure reared up out of the darkness of a broad palmetto, almost sending him into cardiac arrest.

"Taylor, you fucking asshole. Where have you been?"

The man smiled grimly, one arm hanging at his side. His clothes were obviously wet, clinging to his skin. There was a large swath of darkness down his gray t-shirt that Damon assumed was blood.

"I've been fighting for my life, if you can't tell," he said, sarcasm lacing the words.

Damon frowned, not appreciating the snottiness of the tone. "I do see that, but your injuries are the least of our issues tonight. We need to get the fuck out of here before the Secret Service cleans us from the property."

Taylor glanced around warily, then motioned to the left. "This way."

Damon followed him for about ten minutes before they came to a tall stuccoed wall. "We need to get over this."

Damon frowned. It had to be at least ten feet. "And how do we do that exactly?"

"We have to work together. If you cup your hands for me to step in, I can probably get to the top. Then I'll lean over and help pull you over."

Damon scowled, not liking the idea at all. They needed to stay together, though, and this was the only way he could think to get over the obstacle. "Fine," he snapped.

Interlacing his fingers, he tried to brace for Taylor's weight, but it didn't work. Taylor's foot broke through Damon's grip. Resettling, he tried to brace again.

"If I can step on your knee I should be able to do it. Let's try it that way."

Damon braced, not appreciating being used this way. Taylor stepped on him and it was only when he was on top of the wall that Damon realized that he could be left behind. Taylor swung himself around, though, and reached down to brace Damon as he walked up the wall. The stucco hurt and he was so pissed to be in this situation. He took care not to smash the shaving kit or phone. They were the most valuable objects in his possession right now.

They dropped to the opposite side and Taylor took off into a shambling run. This area housed only the most exclusive residents, and there were long expanses of fenced yards and gated drives. They needed to get out of sight.

When a white community security vehicle rounded the corner in front of them, it seemed meant to be. Taylor stepped out onto the street to wave the vehicle down.

An older man with graying hair stopped the SUV and stepped out. "What happened to you guys? Is that blood?"

Taylor slammed into the man and sent him sprawling. Damon heard the man's head crack on the asphalt, but he was already climbing into the passenger side of the vehicle.

————

Elizabeth stared into the night. She wanted to pace, but Wulfe wouldn't let her. So she sat in the over-cologned car they'd stolen and worried at her fingernails.

"You don't want people to notice you."

It was going on midnight, though, and the area at this end of the marina had cleared out significantly. Well it was *Miami*, there was still some partying going on, but it wasn't nearly as busy as it had been before. The marina lights danced merrily, totally mocking her near-panicked mood.

They'd stolen a car as soon as they'd gotten away from the safe house, and she wasn't even sure she knew how he'd done it. It seemed liked Wulfe had just pressed a hand to the door and the locks had popped open. It was like he had the key in his hand. Same with starting the car. It was a newer BMW, but that didn't seem to bother Wulfe. Putting one hand on the ignition, he simply started the car. He shifted the sedan into gear and drove away.

It seemed like he was distracting her when he told her to email Blake, but it worked. She emailed her son and told him that she was coming for him. His response to go to the marina surprised her but made her hope that Noah was still with him.

They waited for almost an hour before a boat idled into the marina. It was long and sleek and made for speed. It pulled up to the public dock and a big man jumped out, securing a rope to the cleat. Then a big black dog jumped to the boards, followed by a young boy.

Elizabeth was out of the car and racing down the dock before she had a chance to think about the repercussions. She snatched Blake up into her arms, tracing her hands all over him. "Are you okay?"

"Mom," he interrupted. "This is Seben. He helped save us. Can we keep him?"

Elizabeth looked down at the dog and shook her head in surprise. The very tall dog had sparkling brown eyes and very white teeth, though the rest of his body was black as night. Large, pointed ears perked up from his head. In the meager light from the marina lights she thought she might have seen the movement of a large tail sweeping back and forth in happy arcs. "Um, we'll see."

"Thanks, Mom!" Blake flung his arms around her neck, apparently interpreting 'we'll see' as *yes*.

Elizabeth glanced up at Wulfe. He had a chiding look on his face.

Turning away, her gaze caught on Noah, and her throat tightened with emotion. There was blood on his face but she couldn't tell where he'd been struck. Stepping close she wrapped her arms around his thick torso. "Thank you so much for taking care of my son. There is no way on earth I can repay you."

"Don't worry about it, ma'am."

He patted her awkwardly on the back before pulling away.

Wulfe rested a hand on her shoulder. "I think we need to get out of here and figure out everything that's happened."

His words had no sooner left his mouth than two black SUVs pulled into the marina. Noah immediately stepped in front of Blake as Seben snapped to attention at his side. Wulfe's hand tensed on her arm as if he were about to drag her away, then relaxed. Officer Rose stepped out of one of the vehicles and approached them.

Wulfe grinned at the man, but Elizabeth shifted guiltily. She'd gone back on her word to him and she needed to apologize. She waited for him to draw close before she spoke. "I hope you'll forgive me, Officer Rose. I couldn't leave my son there."

"I didn't think you would. That's why I tagged your cell phone."

Elizabeth removed her phone from her pocket but couldn't see what he meant. Rose showed her the slim disk on the back of the case. It was barely even visible.

She had to smile at his ingenuity. "Okay, you go me there. Thank you for letting it play out."

The man shrugged. "It was working out. If it had gone sideways we would have stepped in."

Since Noah was the only unknown, she introduced him to the group. "He's been my son's guard for the past two years, and I wouldn't trust Blake with anyone else. Noah, this is Wulfe Terberger and Operations Officer Rose with the CIA."

Noah's dark eyes widened slightly when they rested on Rose. "Sir, I need to brief you on some things."

"Is it time sensitive?"

"Yes, sir."

CHAPTER ELEVEN

They all climbed into one of the SUVs. Rose moved all of his people into the second one so that they could have a semblance of privacy. Elizabeth listened to Noah's account of what happened with fear in her heart. Then growing anger.

"They were going to kill my son?" She hissed, hoping that Blake couldn't hear through the headphones she'd made him put on. He was too busy petting the dog.

"I believe so, ma'am," Noah admitted. "I don't think any of the rest of my team made it out."

"What about Damon?" Wulfe growled.

Noah's dark eyes flicked to him. "I don't know, sir. The guard that was supposed to be protecting him deserted the house."

"So, there's basically a slaughter at the senator's estate right now?"

Noah nodded once. "Yes, sir. I know I killed at least three of the senator's guards trying to get out. From what I overheard it was a big double-cross."

Rose immediately got onto the phone and had a detailed

conversation with someone on the other end, requesting overhead surveillance. There were a bunch of 'yes, sirs' and 'no, sirs', as if he were being very conscious of revealing details. When he hung up he gave them a nod. "We'll have satellite coverage within three minutes."

Elizabeth's brows lifted into her hairline. When he'd said overhead surveillance she'd thought he'd meant planes, helicopters, or drones. Must be nice to control your own satellite.

Blake burrowed into her and she tightened her arms around him. The dog sat on her feet on the floorboard, head on Blake's lap. As if it weren't a difficult enough situation now they had a dog to deal with. A really big dog.

"You said he was making some kind of deal?" Wulfe asked.

Noah's gaze shifted from Wulfe to Elizabeth, and the bottom fell out of her stomach. "What?"

"He was very resentful of you, ma'am. I don't know if you knew that or not."

She snorted. "Of course I did. We haven't had a real marriage for years because of his pettiness."

Noah blinked and looked down at his hands, then back up at Wulfe and Rose who were sitting in the front seat. "I mostly cover Blake, but the other guards talk. He's come up with several ideas on how to get money so that he can get out of the country, including kidnapping his own son."

"What other plans does he have?" Wulfe asked.

"In about fifteen hours he has a meeting somewhere in Miami to auction off Marathon. He has three vials of it. Actually, two. One he gave to the senator."

"Wait," Elizabeth held up a hand. "What the hell is Marathon?"

Noah stared at her as if she'd lost her mind. "It's the enhancement drug the company has been developing. It's the second gen, used for the past year and a half."

Frowning, she looked at Wulfe. "What was your project called? Spartan? This is the follow-up?"

Wulfe nodded.

"Sounds like someone was a Greek history buff."

Elizabeth blinked. "The only one I know into that stuff is Damon. He was always reading books and watching videos. He loved the whole Greek pantheon. Thought they were a superior race."

"The Battle of Marathon was fought by the Persians to overthrow the Greeks," Officer Rose told them. "But the Athenians kicked their asses, basically."

"That kind of narcissism would definitely appeal to Damon. No wonder he chose those names."

She wasn't going to call him her husband anymore. She didn't want to claim any part of him. He had put her son in mortal danger. There would be no more pandering to his selfishness. She looked back at Noah. "So, how the hell has this Marathon been produced in my company without me knowing about it?"

Noah shook his head. "I'm not sure. I think it's made offsite. Not at the main building."

Elizabeth ran a hand over her face. "I have been so oblivious."

Noah grimaced. "I think you've been focused on your son and other things."

She shook her head. "No, that's not going to fly. I've been watching them for the past six months and I haven't noticed anything."

"I know Mattingly ran it up until she died."

The damn woman kept coming up. Between Damon trying to ruin her company, kidnap her son, and leave her holding the bag with the government, she was so over *everything*.

Wulfe caught her gaze and she took solace from the look

in his dark blue eyes. He understood what she was going through and she would like to think he would stand beside her as they waded through all this.

"So, Marathon does what exactly? And who was it tested on?"

Noah sighed and held out a hand. "Mattingly made an offer to the guards to basically double their pay if they took part in the testing. I know there was another version before this one that really put the guys through the wringer. Marathon is a gentler version, but it has operating issues. They said the first one had even more harsh issues."

"No," Wulfe said flatly. "The testing was what killed everyone, not the drug itself."

Noah blinked. "There was testing on us, but it wasn't too bad. A few people had no reaction to the drug whatsoever. Those people were washed out of the program and sent to different parts of the company."

"This was offsite, you said?"

"Yes, in a big, newly built warehouse on the south side of town."

Her fury began to build. "The *Elton building*?"

Noah nodded.

"That... asshole," she sputtered. Elizabeth could feel anger welling up like a volcano within her, boiling hot and ready to erupt.

The Elton Building had been built as an overflow for a project she was spearheading. One of their drug trials had shown amazing results in treating childhood cancer. They had plans to move the project into the building at the beginning of next year. It had been delayed because Damon had told her there were permit and building issues.

Elizabeth wished she could scream. Every revelation and betrayal was like a punch to the gut. That drug could save children's lives, damn it. They needed the dedicated space to expand. Instead he'd indulged his own greed.

"And was there a doctor you were in contact with? Did anyone examine you?"

"There was a Dr. Pell and several nurses. He wasn't anyone I had ever seen in the main campus."

Well, there was that, at least. If it had been one of her fellow research doctors she worked with every day, she would have had an out and out melt down. The violation of trust would have been catastrophic.

A big hand reached out and squeezed her shoulder. Elizabeth looked up into Wulfe's concerned eyes. She wanted to curl up into his arms and bawl, but she didn't have time for all that. She looked down at Blake's head and tears threatened again. *This* was what was important to her. Everything else could be dealt with.

"If you don't mind, ma'am, would you check Blake out? I think his arm might be injured."

Elizabeth pushed Blake up and motioned for him to hold his arms out. He held the right one out and turned it. There was a smear of blood on the meat of his forearm. "Do you have napkins in here?"

Even better, Rose handed her a package of wet naps, the kind that come with messy take-out food. She opened the package, then began wiping the blood away. Wulfe produced a light from somewhere and it allowed her to see a mark on Blake's arm. Barely even a cut, just a pale line where it looked like something had happened, then scabbed over.

Blake pulled the headphones from his ears. "I forgot I got shot," he said, grinning.

Elizabeth felt the blood leave her face and she started turning his arm, looking for an actual bullet hole.

"No, it was right there, Mom. Ah, man, there's no hole. I guess it just nicked me and hit Noah."

The guard shifted under the scrutiny as they all turned toward him. "Are you hit?" Wulfe demanded.

Noah gave a one-shouldered shrug, then winced. "It's not bad. It can wait until we get to where we're going."

That seemed to be a signal to Officer Rose, because they left the marina in haste. It was only a few minutes before they were pulling into the safe-house again and trooping up the walk and into the house that she noticed that Noah wasn't using that arm at all. One of the other agents was an EMT, Rose said, but he was out surveilling the Hall estate.

"I can look at him," she said firmly.

She was a freaking doctor, after all. She laughed internally at the thought. She'd never treated a person in her life, other than her son for the occasional cold or flu.

Noah stripped within a few seconds of getting inside. Elizabeth was aghast at the size of the hole in Noah's infraspinatus muscle, as well as the amount of blood he'd lost. It had run down his back and darkened the back of his pants. Apparently when he'd been carrying Blake, the boy's arm had been in just the right position to be skimmed as Noah was hit.

She realized again how much she owed Noah for saving her son's life. Maybe that was why there'd been so much blood on Blake's arm. It had been from holding onto his wounded guard.

"This is a little more serious than anything I've ever dealt with," she admitted.

Wulfe caught her gaze. "You are the only one here to treat him. You can do it."

The safe house did have a decent medical kit, so she set about gloving up and planning her attack. This was miles outside of her comfort zone but Noah deserved her care. He'd saved her son's life.

After she gave him a hefty shot of lidocaine, she cleaned

and palpated the wound, trying to control her cringing as more blood welled from her touch and he gasped in pain. She was a researcher, not a damn medic. The worst part, though, was when she realized that she could see a glint of metal in the center of the wound. Manipulating a pair of curved hemostatic forceps, she had to dig for the bullet. Eventually, though, she pulled the copper piece free, dropping it to a piece of gauze. Using a fingertip, she gently felt the interior of the wound, searching for possible shards that had split off from the bullet, but it seemed to have remained intact.

She made sure the bleeding was stopped with interior stitches, then closed the wound. It had been literally years since she'd sutured anything, so they weren't perfect by any means, but they were better than nothing. And, looking at Noah's rough back, it was obvious a few lopsided stitches weren't going to bother him.

Finally. She wiped as much of his back as she could with gauze, then bandaged the wound. It was only as she stood that she realized how much pain she'd been in on her knees and kneeling over the patient.

Wulfe stood with her. "Are you okay?"

Elizabeth nodded, but she wasn't really sure about her answer. So much had happened in the past two days that she had no idea which direction she was going or even where she'd been. She'd done more wild things in the past day... Her son was safe now, though. That was the most important thing.

The dog, Seben, had sat attentively at Blake's feet as he watched her work on his guard. Elizabeth had a thought that it might not be appropriate for a nine year old to see a bullet being taken out of a man's shoulder, but he seemed steady enough, and curious enough, that she left him alone. He and Noah had been together a long time. He deserved to see him being cared for.

She looked down at her hands, realizing that they'd just gained a usefulness that she'd never tested before. "I need to go wash up."

There was a powder room just off the central hallway. She locked herself inside and immediately went to the sink to clean off the blood she'd somehow gotten inside the gloves. She glanced at the mirror above the sink and gasped. There was blood on her cheek, like she'd brushed away some hair, distracted. Using some dampened tissue, she wiped it away, then threw it in the toilet.

Then, bracing her hands on the edges of the sink, she stared at herself in the mirror, amazed at what she'd just done. Practicing medicine hadn't actually occurred to her before because she loved the research applications so much more, but she suddenly understood the appeal.

She used the restroom and returned to the living room. Noah slept on his belly on the couch and Blake sat on the floor beside him, the dog sitting in front of him, alert for danger.

Tiredness washed over her suddenly and she swayed on her feet.

"Now that you know they're safe will you relax?" Wulfe asked, cupping her elbow.

She nodded, following along as he sat her in a settee. Suddenly, she was beyond tired, and she knew it was because of all of the emotional stresses that had been piled on her. Lifting her legs up to her side, she leaned against the arm of the couch.

"Wait here and I'll go get you a cup of tea," Wulfe told her.

He wasn't even out of the room before she was asleep.

CHAPTER TWELVE

Wulfe didn't blame Elizabeth for passing out. She'd been holding up remarkably well considering everything that had been flying at her. Plus the stress of her son being missing, then possibly shot.

Kneeling down beside the boy, Wulfe held out his hand. "I don't think we've been properly introduced. My name is Wulfe."

The boy shook his hand. "Blake, sir."

Wulfe smiled slightly at the sir. "Mind if I look at your arm, Blake?"

The boy twisted his right arm so that Wulfe could see it in the light. There was a line of scab but nothing else on the smooth skin. He had seen how much blood there had been.

"Did it hurt?" Wulfe asked.

"It did. It blazed like fire." Blake said twisting his arm look at it. "Actually thought it was going to be worse."

The dog sat beside the boy watching everything Wulfe did very carefully. Wulfe had a feeling that if he made a single wrong move the dog would be all over him.

"How did you get the dog?"

"Well," Blake said, "I met him the first day we were there and he barked at me but only because the trainer made him do it. So I went to go see him in his cage and I saw the collar they put on him that gave him shocks. I took it off and threw it away. And earlier when everything was going crazy, he found us and he saved us from one of the senator's guards. I think the other dog, Sechs, was killed. And he was just as nice as Seben."

The boy's eyes dimmed with sadness. Then they brightened again. "At least I got Seben out."

"True," Wulfe said.

"Is Noah going to be okay?"

Wulfe nodded. "Absolutely. He will be fine. Did you see your dad when you were breaking out?"

Blake shook his head. "Dad's been acting weird for the past couple days. I haven't seen him much. He likes to pretend I don't exist if he can."

"Okay," Wulfe said, his heart aching for the boy.

Blake glanced at his mother asleep on the settee. "He said a lot of really mean things. I mean, I know they haven't been getting along for a long time, but recently it's been really bad. I know Dad misses Ms. Mattingly. I think he might've loved her."

Sighing, Wulfe gave a single tip of his chin. "I think you might be right."

"My mom is awesome," he said. "I don't understand why he wouldn't love her."

Wulfe looked at the settee. "I don't understand either. But we're going to make sure she's taken care of from now on."

Wulfe crossed the room to look down at Noah. The man was laying on his front, his muscular back exposed. Most of the blood was wiped away and Wulfe could see the wound on the shoulder blade. It could've been a devastating wound but Noah had managed to get them out of the situation.

What he also noticed though was that the wound was not as debilitating as expected. Wulfe could tell that it had already begun to heal, the edges beginning to mend. The bleeding had also stopped. He had a feeling that the wound would be healed within a couple days.

Rose had disappeared almost as soon as they reached the house. Wulfe knew the man was constantly monitoring the situation at the senator's house, though he was probably more tired than the rest of them. When he found him in the den, Rose was looking at a flat screen television. Instead of programming there was a view of Senator Hall's house from above. Even from across the room Wulfe could see bodies scattered across the lawn and back patio. There was a lot of movement going on and he could tell there was a massive cleanup effort in progress. Who had the senator called to get this done?

"Who's working with him?" Wulfe asked.

Rose, his arms crossed over his chest, shook his head as he stared at the screen. "I have some idea but I'm waiting for a call back."

"Do you think he has the cooperation of the Secret Service?" Wulfe asked.

Rose ran a hand through his mussed hair. "I have no idea," he said, the frustration evident in his voice. "I really hope not because that will be devastating to the president. The two of them served together in Viet Nam. They've been friends longer than you and I've been alive. I really don't want to be the one to tell him that one of his best friends is the most corrupt of his generation."

Wulfe could understand Rose's trepidation. It wouldn't be a position he would be comfortable in either.

Rose's phone rang in his pocket. Pulling it out, he swiped the screen open. "Yes."

It was a very short conversation. He made a couple of 'mmhmm' sounds, and another 'yes', then he hung up. He glanced at Wulfe. "That's Secret Service doing the cleanup."

Wulfe had suspected so. The Secret Service had been fraught with management issues over the past two years, and this seemed to be another misstep. "How will they justify this?"

Rose shrugged. "They may not need to. Hall has enough friends to cover almost anything up."

"Aren't you going to go over there?"

Rose drew in a deep breath. "Not right now. We're getting enough documentation now with the satellite. I also have a team surveilling them from a distance, logging the cars as they come and go."

His phone rang in his pocket again. "Rose."

Listening intently, he glanced at Wulfe. "Roger that. I'm going to send out another team just to see if they can locate. We're close enough he might not have gotten far."

"Corson!" he called, hanging up.

A competent looking young CIA officer stuck his head in the door.

"Take a car and start canvassing the area. Look for a white private security SUV from the Halls' gated community, occupied times two. If you find it, follow it, but don't attempt to stop it without contacting me."

"Yes, sir," the man said. Wulfe knew they'd all been up for hours but the man looked like he'd just rolled out of bed.

Once Corson disappeared, Officer Rose looked at him. "Two men were spotted walking on the north side of the senator's estate. A security guard stopped to assist and was knocked to the ground, his vehicle stolen. Description matches Wilkes."

Fury surged in Wulfe. "You know he'll come after Elizabeth if he thinks he can."

Rose frowned and shook his head. "I don't think so. I think he'll try to sell the vials of Marathon to the group he set up the meeting with."

"Even though Hall might be working against them?"

Rose had no answer.

Wulfe was torn. He wanted to go out and canvas the neighborhood along with Corson, but he didn't want to leave Elizabeth. Especially considering she was all but unconscious.

The greatest danger was Damon.

"Watch Elizabeth."

Striding out of the room, he headed for the door.

"Do not get into trouble," Rose said.

Wulfe grinned him. "I won't."

Even though he was incredibly tired, as soon as he got into his car with his goal before him, all of that tiredness disappeared. If Wilkes was as close as he thought he was, they couldn't lose this opportunity to find him. If, by chance, he made it out of the country there was a very real possibility that they would never see him again. Granted, that wouldn't be a bad thing, but Damon Wilkes had a lot to account for.

He cast his senses wide, trying to feel for any kind of frantic or panicked feeling. Desperation. Frustration. Wulfe made sure to keep a healthy distance between himself and the senator's estate, though, too. The emotion there would debilitate him.

Wulfe drove for hours, wandering the airport and all major thoroughfares around town. Twice he thought he saw security vans, but they were some other company. By the time he pulled back into the safe house, his eyes were burning with fatigue. Knocking on the door one of the officers let him in.

"Officer Rose is catching a few hours of sleep," the woman said.

Wulfe merely nodded and passed by. Elizabeth was still asleep in the settee. She was curled up like she was chilled, though. Crossing the room to her, he lifted her into his arms and left the room, climbing the stairs tiredly. He wasn't sure what room Blake had been assigned, but he knew where his own room was. He let himself into the room then kicked the door shut behind them. Leaning down, he managed to grasp the blankets and pull them away from the mattress, then he settled her down gently. Elizabeth sighed in her sleep but made no other moves to wake. Reaching out he pulled her shoes from her feet and set them aside. Kicking off his own shoes, he lay down on mattress behind Elizabeth. With her warmth in front of him in the cool room, he pulled the sheet over top of them. He was asleep within seconds.

———

Cameron Hall didn't appreciate being made a fool of. Walking in and seeing the armoire door partially open had been a hell of a shock.

As he looked into his personal safe hidden inside, the one that only he had the combination to, he struggled to rein in his fury. The vial of pale amber liquid was gone. He shifted the black leather planner in hopes it had rolled behind or something, but it hadn't. The cash was there, the bonds—even the ring he planned on giving Victoria for her birthday next month— but no vial.

That backstabbing son of a bitch Wilkes had taken it. He didn't know how or when the tables had turned, but he had to have been the one. No one else knew Damon had given it to him.

His heart began to race in his chest and he turned for his desk chair. He had to sit down before he passed out. These little attacks had been happening more and more frequently recently and one of these days he was just going to keel over dead. Wouldn't that make the majority of the Senate happy?

Cameron had always been a ball buster, pushing things through that would have stalled in the hands of other men. The security of the country, he believed, was stronger for his being one of its administrators. Whether people like him or not, he had always had the best interests of the country he loved and the president he had devoted his life to at heart.

Cameron looked down at the planner still clutched in his hand. If the wrong person got a hold of this it would be a national security fiasco. Everything he'd done over the past 40 years of his career was in these journals. He liked to think of them as the good, the bad, and the ugly. There were as many good deeds logged in the pages as there were shady.

The shady deals had often been more important, with longer reaching effects, than the good deeds. Every single action listed in the pages had been done for his beloved country. As Cameron saw it, his wealth was never a goal of any of his deals, just a by-product, a very pleasant benefit of doing business.

The Marathon program was supposed to have been another notation on the good side, he thought ruefully, but there was a chance it would go down as his biggest fuck up yet.

Cameron looked up at the knock on his door. "Enter."

One of his guards ducked his head in. "Sir, the Secret Service is here."

No sooner had the words left the man's mouth then the door was being pushed open behind him. Secret Service Agent McCullough filled the doorway, a smirk on his face. Cameron had known that this would be difficult but seeing the scorn on McCullough's face made it all the worse.

"So, what are we supposed to do with the mess outside?"

"What you always do, make it go away."

McCullough snorted. "We are not your fairy fucking godmothers, Senator. It's not as easy as you think, getting rid of bodies."

Cameron leaned back in his chair, "Yet you always manage to do it."

McCullough shook his head. "This is a big fucking mess."

"Well, you'd better get started then."

Cameron was used to people looking at him like they'd like to kill him. He'd even had a few people actually try, but none of it bothered him. He would work toward a goal no matter how many opposed him.

"Damon Wilkes needs to be found and silenced."

McCullough's deep-set eyes widened slightly in surprise. Cameron would've chuckled if he'd been alone. It was hard to rattle the longtime agent.

"That's a pretty big job," McCullough said. "It's not like getting rid of a hooker who didn't get you off right. He runs a huge company with a lot of connections. His absence will leave a vacuum."

"He already left his life," Cameron said, "and decided to kidnap his boy when he did."

For the second time in just a few seconds McCullough's face gave away his shock.

"He's a threat I need taken out. The boy is safe."

Well, he thought he was. No body had been found yet.

"And how am I supposed to write this off?" the agent asked incredulously.

Cameron's anger surged." I don't give a fuck how you do it, just do it."

McCullough seemed to sense how close to the edge he was, because he tipped an imaginary cap. "Yes, sir."

After the man left, Cameron rested his head back against the chair, incredibly tired. It had been a long day and an even longer night. Maybe while they were cleaning up he would get a few hours of sleep. Did he have the energy to go up and kiss Victoria good night? Not really. Crossing to the office door, he engaged the lock, then did the same with the French doors to his right. There had been no attack in his office, so it wouldn't need to be cleaned. Dropping down to the leather couch on the far wall, he propped his feet up on the arm and stuffed a cushion beneath his head.

CHAPTER THIRTEEN

Elizabeth woke to an incredible warmth seeping through her bones. Yes, they were in Florida, but this was a different kind of warmth. She knew it was Wulfe before she turned her head and for a moment anxiety clutched her stomach. She'd never been presented with a temptation like Wulfe. Her marriage vows had always been inviolable. When she'd married Damon she'd had hopes that it would be a long marriage of mutual respect like her parents had. Even though he hadn't stuck to that tenet of marriage, she had.

She'd never loved Damon though. At twenty-two she had married him out of family obligation. There had been no love involved, not then and not since. She had respected her parents enough to take their guidance when it came to choosing a husband. If she could've gone back and told her twenty-four-year-old self how much of a mess the marriage would turn out to be she would choose a different path. Maybe if she had married Wulfe as she'd dreamed so many times, things would've been different.

No, she couldn't think that way. She would suffer through 50 years of marriage just to have her Blake.

Wulfe shifted and she knew she needed to move. Sitting up, she swung her legs to the side. Just as she was about to stand, Wulfe reached for her hand. "Don't go yet."

His voice had a beautiful morning texture and she was still. She didn't want to leave either, but she felt obligated to. If Blake happened to walk into the room she didn't know how she would explain sleeping with Wulfe. Yes, they had their clothes on, but it would still be one of those *how to explain this to a nine year old* situations she preferred to avoid at the moment. As she turned her head to look into Wulfe's languorous gaze, her determination evaporated. There was a look in his eyes that made her feel like more of a woman than she'd ever been. Wulfe had always had the ability to make her feel like more than she actually was. When everyone else criticized her, he built her up. His support for the few weeks they'd been together had lasted her through the years, building solid memories that no one had been able to tear down.

As he tugged on her hand she didn't fight him the way she needed to. She allowed him to pull her down beside him and when he wrapped his arms around her she allowed herself to absorb the bliss, just for a moment.

"We shouldn't do this, Wulfe."

Wulfe pulled her tighter against him and buried his nose in her hair. As his breath drifted through the strands, she shivered. She cursed her weakness to him. Wulfe had always been able to change her mind, and this was a perfect example.

Then one hand drifted down her arm to cup her hand in his own. She shuddered just from that one small touch. The pads of his fingers lingered on her skin, and she could feel every individual one, in the scrape of the ridges on his fingerprints. They tickled the baby fine hairs on her own fingers.

Wulfe had always known what to do disable her defenses. It was what made him so dangerous to her heart.

No, she couldn't do this right now. She had to remember what they were here for.

Forcing herself to pull away, she stood at the side of the bed. "We need to see what's going on downstairs."

Before she could change her mind, she turned and left the room. The vision of him sleep tussled and warm refused to leave her though.

Walking down the hallway she listened for Blake's voice. When she didn't hear him she headed downstairs. Most of the group were in the kitchen, including her son. He sat next to Noah, grinning and laughing like nothing had happened. Spotting her in the doorway he crossed the room to her to give her a hug.

"I wondered where you were," he said.

"I'm not sure exactly where I was sleeping," she admitted.

"Want some breakfast?"

Elizabeth looked at the spread on the table. "Maybe in a bit."

Instead she crossed to the coffee maker and poured a steaming mug, lowering her head to inhale the steam. There was a bottle of creamer beside the station and she tipped some in. She almost poured the second cup for Wulfe, but decided he could get his own when he came down.

Officer Rose was nowhere to be seen so she headed back to the den area where they'd been strategizing. She found him in what had originally been the living room of the house. There was a flat screen TV broadcasting pictures, but Rose's attention was on the computer screen in front of them at the desk. He looked up when she walked in.

"Mrs. Wilkes," he greeted. "Did you sleep well?"

She grimaced. "Well, after I passed out in front of everyone I don't remember much of anything. I don't even remember how I got upstairs."

Rose shrugged. "I think Wulfe carried you upstairs."

His dark eyes watched her for a reaction but she was determined not to give it to him.

"So, what's going on?" she said, trying desperately to get him to shift his attention.

"Well, it looks like Senator Hall has covered his ass again, this time with the help of the Secret Service. We've been scanning all the local and national news channels and no one has said a word about what happened at his estate last night. Also," he said glancing at her, "we had a sighting of Damon escaping, apparently with one of the guards. I had a couple of people looking for him and Wulfe went out as well, but he wasn't seen again."

Elizabeth deflated in the chair. "So he's going to lie low until he can sell those vials."

"Seems like it," Rose agreed.

"I wish I knew what was in those vials," Elizabeth murmured thoughtfully. "Do we have access to a lab?"

Rose looked at her little oddly. "I can get one if we need one."

Elizabeth shrugged. "I'm just curious. If Noah would give me a sample of his blood maybe I can see what the Marathon drug looks like."

"Not a bad idea. Or, now that you have your son back, you can head back to Arlington. We don't necessarily need you here now."

Hmm. She acknowledged the validity of the suggestion but wasn't sure she wanted to leave. Why *wouldn't* she want to leave? Not because Damon was here. Because Wulfe would probably stay to try to apprehend him.

For the sake of her son, though, she would go back to Virginia. His safety was more important than anything. And if she went back to work she could investigate Marathon. Her lab was the best option to study it anyway. The Collaborative had the most state of the art equipment available. It would certainly make her life easier. Board members were already calling her, asking what was going on. "I think I will head back to Virginia. Then you can focus on bringing these men in. What are you going to do about the senator?"

Rose grimaced and she realized he was still in a bit of an odd position with her. "I understand if you can't tell me. Technically, I *am* possibly the enemy."

Sighing, the man crossed his arms over his chest as he stared at her. She could appreciate that he was torn. Eventually he came to some kind of decision. "I'm not even sure," he said with a sigh. "I'm going to run it up the ladder and see what my bosses say. I have a feeling we'll sit tight and monitor the situation right now, let the Secret Service dig their own grave. They've been getting caught being dirty a lot recently and there are a few key personnel we want to catch."

"I don't envy you your position."

Rose laughed. "I don't either actually. I was handed this position and told to deal with it."

Wulfe came in then and her gaze settled on him. After a night of sleeping in his clothes he should have looked rumpled, but he totally didn't. He looked tall and strong and deliciously appealing. A shiver rippled through her at the remembered pleasure from so long ago.

Wulfe's gaze slammed to hers and his irises darkened, as if he were responding to her body's cues.

Maybe it was a good idea for her to return to Arlington, if just to get away from the temptation.

Wulfe didn't seem pleased when Rose told him the plan. He scowled dangerously, then seemed to realize the danger they could be leaving behind. His face settled into a resigned frown. "Yes, maybe it is best you leave here for now."

Elizabeth tried not to be hurt by the words she herself had spoken, repeated to her. It would be smart to put some distance between herself and Wulfe, as well as Damon and the senator. She knew that.

"Go pack your bag," Rose told her, "and I'll let the pilot know that you're coming."

The bottom dropped out of her stomach as she realized she would have to leave Wulfe behind. No more big, strong German to reinforce her flagging confidence. Then anger surged in her belly, at her own thoughts. Over the past several years, she'd learned to rely on herself for everything. Why did she want to rely on a man now?

Not *a* man, her conscience told her. *The man*. The man who'd taught her everything about being a woman.

Her eyes connected with his and he let her see the frustration he was fighting. He didn't want her to leave either. But it would be best for all of them. "You need to find Damon," she told him firmly. "He is a continued threat to so many people. If another country gets those vials there could be a very real possibility the security of the nation could be at risk."

Rose nodded in agreement. "Wulfe will stay here with me. Ms. Wilkes, *Doctor* Wilkes," he said, somewhat startled. "I just realized that we haven't been addressing you correctly."

Elizabeth smiled in appreciation. "Thank you. I seldom use the title, but I appreciate the consideration."

"I'll have a team meet you in Arlington. Perhaps as a way to show your... cooperation with the federal government, I'll send you some of the men we've rescued. Perhaps you can gain some insight into this mess."

Elizabeth scowled. "I will, of course, but on one condition that is absolutely non-negotiable. Those men have to be *completely* willing, without threat or coercion, to work with me. I won't do anything by force or by intimidation or anything underhanded. I don't work that way, no matter how it looks for my company, the government, or anyone else right now."

Rose looked at Wulfe for a long moment, then angled his head to her. "I agree. And I thank you for that consideration. I would never have forced them, but I appreciate your clarification."

Elizabeth felt a knot of tension ease in her chest. In the back of her mind she must have been anticipating a situation like this. She'd known that at some point her loyalty would be tested. "And, just to clarify, what are the goals of this research? What's the end game?"

Sighing, Rose planted his hands on his hips. "I don't think we have a specific end game yet, but if we mess up and another country gets their hands on those vials, and it enhances the men like it has others," he waved a hand at Wulfe, "then we need to be prepared to fight that somehow. We need to know the breakdown of the serums that they've used to enhance the men. Then we need a protocol in place in case enhanced soldiers are used against us."

"You don't ask for much, do you?" Elizabeth sighed. "You realize that the scope of the issue could be much bigger than I can get a handle on."

"I do. But I also know that you have made a name in your own right on the quality of your work, and your determination to see projects through. I know about your Elton project, as well as several other long-running programs you're invested in."

Yeah, he would know that. If her company had been under investigation for as long as she thought it had, he would probably know everything he possibly could about it. For a moment, she felt very exposed. Some of those programs were very dear to her heart. Some of those programs she'd pumped a lot of money into, though she hadn't gotten much return. She let the patented drugs the company had created carry them financially, while she pursued the more challenging, less appreciated diseases. Working in her lab had been a freedom she'd never experienced anywhere else. Now she would have to shift her focus to Marathon, and try to dig the company out of the hole Damon had put them in. She wasn't sure when it had all began to go sour, but she should have been paying more attention. This would now be her responsibility to shoulder. If she had any hope of salvaging her family's company, she would have to take this on.

"Then I agree to the collaboration."

Rose held out a hand and they shook. "Although I will have to send a couple people to work with you and oversee your research."

Elizabeth's smile faltered, but she should have expected some kind of oversight. "I'm going to refocus my team to work on this. I have two more doctors as well as several research assistants that are top notch, but I need to know how much I can tell them."

"Tell them only what you have to. One of the people rescued from the Brazilian camp was a nurse. As the men were being tested upon, she was caring for them at night and trying to reverse some of the effects."

"Oh," Elizabeth breathed. "She would be incredibly helpful, then, if she's willing to work with us."

Rose pulled his phone from his pocket and began writing out a note on the screen. "Let me make a few calls with my boss and I'll see what I can do while you're in the air."

Elizabeth knew a dismissal when she heard one so she turned to go. Wulfe followed her out of the room. Feeling the need for privacy, she led him through the house and back up to his bedroom. Her heart began to pound as she led him inside.

Needing something to do she crossed to the mattress and began making the bed. "I think it will be good for us to take a

breather from each other. As much as I appreciate everything
you've done for me, I have to get my ass in gear and start to
get this situation straightened out. It's my fault those men
died and were treated so horribly. This is my chance to try to
make it better. To try to keep the family name from going
down in the history books as one of the most evil companies
ever..."

She swiped at her wet cheeks, not even realizing when
she'd started crying.

Wulfe gripped her shoulders from behind and turned her
to face him. He let out a rumble when he saw her face. He
tilted her chin up with his thumb, forcing her to look at him.
"It is not your fault, Elizabeth. It never was. Damon made the
choices he did because he is greedy. Not you."

"No, I know that, but I should have been keeping a better
eye on my family's company. I was content to sit in my little
gilded lab and tinker and let him run everything. Me, the
company, my child." She shook her head, anger surging in her
gut and she pulled away from his touch. "No more, damn it.
I'm not rolling over and taking the easy way out any more.
I'm going to stand up for what I want and what I believe in,
and I'm going to get my company going in the direction it
needs to be."

Elizabeth hated that she'd resorted to cursing, but sometimes polite words just ran out. Wulfe was grinning at her,
dark brows raised over his eyes. He was so handsome
standing there. It had made her heart ache leaving him in bed
earlier. If she had her choice...

She stopped her thoughts abruptly. It would do no good
bemoaning what had happened if she didn't work to change
her situation. Then, because she was testing out a theory, she
stepped into his personal space and tipped her chin up,
meeting his eyes. Wulfe sighed, reaching out to cup her head
and angle his lips over hers.

Ten years ago she'd been innocent and eager, and he'd taken incredible care with her. She'd worried that being in the research camp would have changed him, but he was just as eager and careful as he'd been then. Her heart raced as he made a sound low in his throat, like she had stroked a memory. Cupping his face in her hands she played with the beard stubble that shadowed his jaw, appreciating the intimacy.

Wulfe wrapped a hand around her neck, and his second hand went down low over her hips, teasing the swell of her bottom. Immediately, a wash of heat rolled through her lower body, and parts of her began to tingle. He had always affected her like this, quick and hard. And she could feel that he was just as affected. She angled her hips into his hard length, wishing she had the freedom to go further.

Then, reluctantly, she drew back. He held her for a moment, as if he didn't want to let her go, then he forced his hands open.

Elizabeth wanted to cry again, but she forced the tears away. He had always done what she wanted, even if it hurt himself. Looking up she met his turbulent blue eyes. "It was as perfect as I remember. And it gives me hope, Wulfe, that when this mess is over we can finally be together. Can you wait for me? As much as I hate Damon right at this moment I won't ignore my marriage vows. It wouldn't be fair for anyone and it wouldn't give Blake a good impression of either of us. It certainly wouldn't be fair to you."

His great chest expanded with a sigh, and he nodded. "I understand. And my head says you do a good thing, but my heart..." he grimaced, resting a hand over his chest. "Yes, I will wait for you to be free, Elizabeth. I've waited ten years already."

Throat closing off with emotion, she went into his arms, tucking her head beneath his chin. "One of these days we'll be able to be our own people. You know? I'm so tired of not being me, of tamping that woman down for convention."

She felt him press a kiss to her hair. "You don't need to tamp her down for me. I like the wild and crazy Liz."

She giggled, pulling back to look up into his laughing eyes. "Wild and crazy, huh? I don't ever remember being that way."

"Let's finish with Damon and we'll get you there."

She took that as a promise for a future, and her determination resolved.

CHAPTER FOURTEEN

Damon looked at the phone in his hand and grinned, then slipped it into his pocket after he cleared the notification. That was exactly what he needed to know.

Someone had turned Blake's cell phone back on and the GPS was reporting again. Blake, and more importantly, his backpack, were only a few miles away. He glanced at the time in the right hand corner. Almost seven a.m.

He sat up on the side of the bed, his back aching from the sag in the middle of the mattress. They'd only had a few hours of sleep and it hadn't been great sleep, but it was going to have to do. They had things to do today.

He looked at the other bed. Taylor still slept, his bad shoulder open to the air. It had quit bleeding hours ago and as Damon blinked, he could see where the wound had begun to knit together. That was amazing.

No, *Marathon* was amazing and he planned on using Taylor as a visual aid at the meeting later today. What a great pitch. "This soldier was shot last night, but you can't tell today! Imagine entire armies coming back from the brink of death!"

What would Marathon do for *him* if he took an injection? He was athletic, but it was more of a Sunday afternoon tennis type of athletic, or showing up at the gym for an early meeting. He'd certainly never had any kind of military training. He doubted a shot of it would do him any good at all. It was a little tempting though, as he looked at the way Taylor had recovered.

Standing, he arched his back and strained, popping joints as his body settled back into realignment. This motel was a very long step down from what he was used to, but they'd accepted cash and hopefully there wouldn't be any way to track them. He had no doubt that Senator Hall had people looking for him, if just to confirm his life or death. Damon was a very big loose end. The senator was probably shaking in his boots wondering when the media would come pounding on his door.

For a moment Damon wondered if that wasn't something he should consider, going public. The senator was a much bigger fish than he was. If the federal government would give him a break, he would consider it. Yeah, he seriously doubted it would happen, but it might be an option to be kept in the back of his mind. For now he would hang out for a few hours then send out the email that had been prearranged. He had delegates from Mexico, Brazil, Venezuela, Iran and Yemen meeting him at a shuffleboard park in downtown Miami in eight hours. They would coordinate phone calls and the drug would go to the highest bidder. It was that easy. He didn't care about their current turmoil and even that Venezuela and Brazil had helped him out tremendously over the past two years with the camps, he couldn't be partial if it meant he was losing money.

Taylor would escort him and as soon as they were done and the money in his hand, they would be chartering a plane to France. Sometime this afternoon he would call his contact there and feel him out. If the extradition deal wasn't going to fly then he would have to come up with alternate plans.

———

Elizabeth stared out the window at the rising Florida sun. It was stunning. Even in the midst of the chaos of her life right now she could still appreciate the beauty. She looked over at the bed. Blake slept there, his face peaceful, not showing any of the strain of the past few days. She wasn't even sure he was aware that he had been kidnapped by his father. He thought they'd just taken a trip to see the senator as they had done before. Seben slept beside him, although she thought he was aware of her moving around. One bat-like ear had wiggled as she crossed the room to the window.

As beautiful as it was here, she would be glad to be getting as far away from Damon and the senator as she could. It would be a relief to be back in her own home. That reminded her. She needed to contact the house staff to let them know that their situation had changed with Damon's... defection. And Alicia, her already-overworked assistant, would have to know everything, just in case Elizabeth missed something important. The door locks would need to be changed as well as the alarm codes. Everything in the house would need to be changed. The thought was daunting.

Even more daunting was the thought of taking over the company. It would have to be done though. Hopefully there were enough loyal people to guide her as she took over. All of the major players in the company were either dead, missing, or on the lam. She snorted softly, wondering how on earth her life had changed so drastically.

She's supposed it didn't really matter. Life had thrown a punch at her and she needed to get up off the ground to fight back.

Crossing to the bureau she withdrew the change of clothes that Blake would have to wear home today. They weren't exactly his sizes but they would do. She didn't ask Officer Rose where he'd gotten them, just thanked him politely and promised she would be ready for the morning flight.

Crossing to the bed she shook Blake's shoulder gently. He sighed and rolled over, one hand automatically going to pet the dog. It was startling how connected they were after only a few hours of being together.

"Blake, you need to go get in the shower."

"Ah, Mom," he grumbled. "Can't I sleep a little more?"

"You can sleep on the plane," she told him softly. "Come on."

He rolled out of the bed and padded to the bathroom, Seben on his heels. The dog would have to go out himself at some point.

Gathering up his dirty clothes she folded them and set them on the bed, then began winding the chargers for his tablet and his phone. Something thumped against her leg as she picked up his backpack and she looked inside curiously. School papers that should have been thrown away months ago, pens, some kind of little Japanese toy that changed shapes. Then there was a black case she didn't recognize. Frowning, she unzipped the case and unfolded it. Inside, resting on a black cushion with a piece of elastic around it was a vial of golden liquid. What the hell?

Icy fear rolled through her as she realized what she held. This had to be Marathon. Why the hell was it in her son's bag, though? Had he picked it up somewhere? No. It had to be because Damon had expected to keep Blake with him.

She looked up at the knock on her door, fear surging in her. What would they think when they found her in possession of the formula? After all her protestations of innocence, she now had the instrument of evil literally in her hands.

─────

Cameron woke to the feel of soft hands on his forehead and cheeks, and the scent of coffee on the air. He blinked his eyes open and looked up at Victoria, backlit by the morning in a stunning halo. She looked glorious, truly breathtaking and fresh as she leaned down to press a kiss to his lips. Cameron smiled in spite of himself, then the previous night began to drift back to him.

"Are our guests gone?" Cameron asked.

Victoria nodded once. "I don't know what went on here last night, and I'm not going to ask, but everything is clean. Other than a few nicks out of the marble and some missing people, it's the same as yesterday."

Cameron sat up on the couch, making her shift back. He was still in his office, he saw. Then he turned look at her. "How did you get in here?"

Positioning her head to the side, Victoria gave him a speaking glance. "Your office doors were standing wide open this morning."

Scowling, he looked at the heavy oak door and the electronic lock. There should've been no way for the door to be open other than by his own hand. He glanced at Victoria, wondering if she had somehow developed the knowhow to jimmy the lock. No, he thought, looking at her curling golden hair, electronics were not Victoria's forte. It seemed more likely to be a shot across his bow by McCullough. He could see the man having the personnel to get through his security, then leaving the door open just to remind Cameron that he wasn't the only strong arm in the game. Asshole. As soon as they got through this mess he would be looking into getting rid of the longtime agent. There had to be something in his background he could exploit.

"I brought you a cup of coffee."

Without a word he stood and dropped a kiss to her lips. Then, crossing to his desk he reached for the mug, his mind kicking into gear. Damon had escaped last night and Cameron needed to find the lying pig. Somehow he'd gotten the vial of drug out of his safe and he wasn't sure how.

Luckily, he hadn't made any concrete plans to use the drug. The invasion chafed, though, and made him second-guess the security he had in place. What else did he have wrong?

Victoria smiled at him as she left the office.

CHAPTER FIFTEEN

Wulfe didn't notice anything amiss when he let himself in through the door. He'd knocked, but by the alarmed look on Elizabeth's face she hadn't heard him. She looked shocked, and guilty, more so than warranted by the surprise. Then he looked at what she held in her hands and his blood froze in his veins.

Though he hadn't heard a description of the drug, he had to assume that this was Marathon. The vial was only about four inches long, but he could clearly see the honey gold liquid inside. It looked similar to the original. The concentration of the Ayahuasca root in the Spartan program had been a darker color, though, more of an amber ale rather than a lager.

His gaze flicked up to Elizabeth's and he was taken aback to see cold determination in her expression. "No matter what you think," she told him harshly, "this is not mine. This was in the bottom of Blake's backpack. Damon must have put it there in the hopes that we wouldn't find it. I just this second reached into the bag and pulled it out when you knocked and came in."

Wulfe stepped forward to her, taking the vial from her pale fingers. He could feel the righteous anger in her body, and the fear that he would think it was hers. He could also feel the bigger fear that it could all fall apart in this second, and he felt like it was directed at him and their relationship.

Smiling slightly, he rolled out reassurance. Her body softened immediately. "Don't worry, *mein liebchen*. I know it's not yours. Ease yourself."

When he wrapped his arm around her she melted into him, crying softly. "I couldn't look much guiltier," she said softly, exhaling tension from her body.

"No," he chuckled, "you couldn't. I could feel you weren't being... underhanded. I don't think you can be. You don't have the face for it."

She looked up at him, tears in her eyes, and he had to lean down and kiss her.

"Uh, Mom?"

She tried to jerk away guiltily but Wulfe held onto her hand. He turned to face Blake.

The boy gave him a bit of a sideways glance, as prideful as he could be wrapped in only a towel. "What am I supposed to wear?"

Elizabeth pulled her hand away and reached for the stack of clothing on the bed. "May not be exactly your size but it's close enough."

He took the clothing in one hand and headed back into the bathroom, but not before giving Wulfe a dark look.

After the door closed, Wulfe chuckled lightly. "He doesn't know what to think."

Elizabeth gave him an equally dark look. "Well, of course not," she told him. "He's only just met you. He has no idea the history we have."

Wulfe wanted to tell her that there would be a future as

well but he didn't think she was ready to hear that. Maybe once all of this was over with.

"I hate to see you go," he admitted.

She looked up at him, her blue eyes shadowed with worry. "I know, but I really do think it's best. Blake has to be my priority, above even my needs and wants."

He didn't say anything. His head thought it was a good idea, but his instincts were telling him to keep her with him. "Now that you have that will it make it easier?"

She looked down at the vial as she took it from him. "Oh my gosh, yes. I'm hoping, too, that once I get back to Arlington I'll be able to get into Damon's computer and files. I need to meet with the board and have a long talk about the direction of the company, and I need to figure out which one of them knew what was going on. Or maybe all of them. They were all contemporaries of my father so I'm sure I'll get some kind of convoluted answer that will be too much for my female mind to understand."

"Stick to your guns," he told her, lightly resting a finger over her chest. "You know in here what's right or wrong."

She nodded, looking down at the fluid. She rocked it back and forth in her hand, seemingly mesmerized. "It's amazing to me what people will do for this. And this is the lesser variation, right?"

He nodded. "The serum we were given was a different recipe. There are several different variations of the Ayahuasca root, and even some regional differences within the varieties. Dr. Shu always wrote the recipe down, but it was only later, according to his journal, that he realized the region that the root was collected from had such a strong impact on the final product. So, even though the way he made it was the same, the ingredients changed the final abilities of the subjects."

Her expression turned wary. "So, can I ask you exactly

what you can do? It may give me a control to keep in mind as I start breaking down Marathon."

Wulfe wondered if she realized how worried she looked. Theoretically she was okay with his enhanced abilities. She'd given him a few odd looks here and there, but she hadn't been alarmed. But then, she had only seen a fraction of what he could do.

"I can read and manipulate the emotions of others, at times. A few minutes ago you were swamped in guilt and you thought I would see you as complicit with Damon and the company."

She nodded, lips parted and her eyes wide.

"I sent out a wave of reassurance because I could *feel* that you weren't guilty. I'm not sure if you noticed or not."

She shook her head, brow furrowing. "I knew that one minute I was sure you were going to hate me, then the next I knew you were going to be okay with it. And we were going to be okay."

He dipped his chin to her. "Exactly. I have to be within fifty feet to affect emotions effectively, so to speak. Distance dissipates the effect. If I am in a hostile situation I can blast an emotion at a suspect, stunning them." He shrugged. "I have a natural affinity to water, even more than when I was in the navy. I can change the temperature and density of it. Since the human body is mostly water, I can manipulate it the way I need to in order to gain the advantage in a fight."

Her mouth dropped open. "That's amazing. I had no idea."

"I can also manipulate electricity if I'm in close proximity. Fontana is the one who is amazing. He can look at something from thirty feet away and blow it up. We all came out of the testing with different abilities. I talked with Aiden this morning, told him a bit of what was going on."

She held up a hand. "Aiden was one of the ones you escaped with?"

"*Ja.* Aiden, Fontana, myself, and one other. He died a while ago, killed by one of Mattingly's enhanced operatives, and it affected us all."

Wulfe looked out over her head. TJ had been a good friend, and his loss had been harsh. Wulfe had felt his death even though he'd been hundreds of miles away. It had rippled through the air, then through his mind, sending him reeling. Aiden had been right there with him and it was no wonder the man's mind had broken for a while.

"We are the Dogs of War. It was what TJ named us, because we were dogs in a Silverstone cage, and we vowed when we broke out that every single person, company, entity attached to the torture would be taken down."

Tears filled her eyes but she didn't let them fall. "I hate that my family's legacy of bringing hope and relief to so many people has been corrupted. I'm so sorry. If I ever meet your friends you can be sure I will tell them the same thing. I'm so sorry I let the company go. When I was a kid I had planned to take over my father's legacy. It was in the back of my mind for as long as I can remember. It was why I did the dual degrees in college. But when the time came, my father just didn't have the confidence in me to take over the company. I think partially because of our affair."

Wulfe nodded. He'd assumed that as well. "You were like me. We listened to our parents and did as we were told, but I couldn't do that where you were concerned. There was just something about you that I couldn't deny." He ran a finger down her cheek. "And there still is."

Elizabeth wavered on her feet, like she wanted to lean forward and kiss him again but he held up a finger, glancing pointedly at the bathroom. Leaning down close to her ear, he whispered, "We have an observer."

Pulling back he grinned down at her. "I was the same as a child. If you wanted to learn anything in my household you had to sneak around like a mouse."

She nodded, humor taking light in her pale, too serious eyes. "Mine as well. And I had a nanny that used to tell me things no one else would."

Wulfe nodded and mouthed 'watch' to her. "Yes, that's all well and good, but I don't think Noah is a good guard. He's reckless and obviously has no control over the boy."

There was the sound of scrambling, then the bathroom door was jerked open. Blake lurched out, furious frown on his face. "Noah is my guard and he's not going anywhere, no matter what you say. Mom, tell him."

Wulfe glanced at Elizabeth and they chuckled. Then she turned to her son, a stern look settling on her face. "We just said that because we knew you were listening. Noah is an excellent guard. He's not going anywhere. However, you need to be aware that eavesdropping is bad. When you hear bits and pieces you don't always see the entire puzzle."

Blake looked down at his well-worn shoes. "I understand, ma'am, but sometimes it's the only way I learn anything. No one actually tells me anything, other than Noah, and I'm old enough to know what's going on."

Folding her arms over her chest, Elizabeth regarded him critically. "I agree that you are old enough to know some things, but you have to be content that there are some things we will not talk to you about. Adult stuff."

"Like the torture Dad was letting go on? I saw some of the pictures," he admitted, voice barely above a whisper.

Immediately, Elizabeth crossed the room to kneel at his side. "You saw pictures? When?"

The boy shrugged his narrow shoulders, looking guilty. "It's was a couple of months ago, back when Ms. Mattingly got back from one of her trips. I was waiting for you to get done in the lab and I got bored, so I started wandering around. I heard her say something about progress, then she started giggling and they talked about other things." For some reason he looked even guiltier at that second, a flush working up his cheeks, and Wulfe wondered if he hadn't overheard them having sex or something. "Later, I snuck in and there were pictures on the desk, just laying out for everyone to see. There were men on there, but they had cuts and stuff on them. I think one guy was actually dead," he whispered.

Elizabeth wrapped him into her arms and held him to her. "I'm sorry, honey. You shouldn't have had to see or hear that. I'm glad you told me about it."

Pressing a kiss to his forehead she pulled back. "Your dad has been doing some bad things with the company. He's developed a drug to try to create soldiers that are physically better than the regular military, but it doesn't work right. I'm going to tell you something big, Blake, and I want you to think about it and ask me questions later. Okay?" She waited for his nod. "Your dad kidnapped you to bring you down here, and he's made a bunch of other bad decisions. He's trying to sell the newest version of the drug to make a bunch of money."

Blake nodded, his eyes lighting. "To the people from Mexico and Brazil. I heard him talking about it to the senator."

Wulfe stepped forward, alarmed. "What else did you hear, Blake? This is very important. Did he say where they were meeting?"

Blake blinked. "At some kind of park. It's a sport but it sounded like something old people did. My dad laughed about it but the senator said it wasn't so bad."

"Golf?"

Blake shook his head. "No, it was two words. I know golf."

"Bocce ball?" Elizabeth asked.

The boy shook his head again. "Old people do it when they retire."

"Tennis?"

Blake scowled. "No, I can't think of the name of it. It was kind of funny though."

Wulfe looked at Elizabeth, considering. They'd listed the most popular ones.

"Shuffleboard?" Elizabeth asked, grasping at straws now.

"Yeah, that's it! Shuffleboard. I thought it was funny because I could see people shuffling to play it."

Elizabeth grinned at his imagination. "Do you remember if he said where?"

"Downtown Miami, somewhere."

Wulfe drew out his phone and began tapping through screens. There were shuffleboard parks all over Miami, but the biggest one was at a park in the city center. "You remember him talking about Mexico and Brazil. Are you positive about that, Blake?"

"Yes, I remember those two, but there were others that he listed, too. At least three more. And he told the senator that if the deal worked out the way he wanted he would be sipping wine in France in no time."

Wulfe made note of everything the boy said. France was a bit of a surprise. They were not as militaristic as the other countries he'd listed, but the government had money to spend. Wulfe ran through the countries in his head, wondering if Blake would recognize the names. "Yemen?"

Blake nodded. "I think so. And there was one that started with a V."

"Venezuela?"

"Yes! And Mexico. I remember that one because I just did a report on it for school. But there was another one."

Wulfe thought about the Middle East. They would jump on something like this. "Iraq or Iran?"

"Um, I think one of those. Not sure which one."

"That's okay. They're both bad."

Wulfe looked at Elizabeth. "I need to go talk to Officer Rose. This is pretty big. Do you mind if we go talk to him with Blake?"

She nodded, understanding in her expression. "What should I do with this?"

She held up the vial.

"I would put it back into the case and guard it with your life. I think that is very valuable." Then something occurred to him and his blood chilled. "How many vials were in that case?"

She flipped the black leather open. "There are spaces for three."

"Three," Blake confirmed.

They turned to look at him. "You saw the vials?"

"Yes, there were three of them. It was in Dad's safe at the office before we left on the plane."

Elizabeth looked shell shocked. Wulfe thought it was pretty funny, though. They'd learned more from a nine year old boy in the past few minutes than they had in the past few days of surveillance and interrogation. "We need to go talk to Officer Rose. Elizabeth, put that vial in the case and bring it with you."

CHAPTER SIXTEEN

They trooped down the stairs and into Officer Kevin Rose's makeshift office in the den of the safe house. Wulfe related the most pertinent information, making sure that Rose understood the source. He looked at the boy askance, grinning softly.

"Doesn't it figure," he said softly. Reaching out he shook Blake's hand. "I appreciate what you've told us young man. You don't have any idea about what time your dad was supposed to meet them, do you?"

Blake made a face. "It was in the middle of the day, I think, but I don't remember him or his guards saying an exact time."

The three of them shared a look. Rose lifted his wrist. "It's going on eight, now. I'm going to get a couple of teams going across the city and see what we can see."

"I want to help," a voice said from the doorway.

Noah stood there looking strong and ready, like he'd never even been shot.

"Are you okay, Noah?" Elizabeth asked, moving toward him.

"Yes, ma'am. I've been hurt worse than just a single bullet."

She flinched and Wulfe realized she thought because of the drug. "Noah used to be in the Marines, yes?"

Noah glanced at him and nodded. "Yes, sir. Did four tours in Iraq and Afghanistan. A bullet in the shoulder blade is nothing."

Wulfe appreciated the steadiness of the man. He was a good guard for Blake, and he seemed loyal to the boy rather than who signed his paychecks. "Did you even think about going back into the house to find Damon?"

The man blinked, his dark eyes flat. "No, sir. Damon is not my principal."

Wulfe grinned and moved forward to shake his hand. "We didn't get a chance to talk much last night, but I think you and I are going to get along well."

Noah gave him a half-smile, then turned to Blake with a full smile as the boy stepped up for a hug around Noah's middle.

"Are you okay, Noah?"

"I'm totally fine, I swear."

The boy looked skeptical, and the guard seemed to sense that he needed reassurance. "Look."

Noah turned his back to them and peeled the olive green t-shirt up over his shoulders to drape around his neck. Wulfe noted the numerous scars over his back, and the most recent higher on his shoulder blade. Even Elizabeth stepped forward to stare in amazement at the healed skin. Noah's very dark skin showed pink in a circle where the bullet had hit, but it looked a couple of weeks old rather than a day old. Elizabeth ran her fingers over the stitches she herself had placed and shook her head.

"Damn," she whispered softly.

Blake's gaze jerked to her, his eyes huge in his face. "Mom, you cussed! You never cuss!"

She made a face. "I have over the past couple of days, O son of mine."

Blake grinned at her. "That's okay. You're allowed."

Elizabeth grinned back at him, pale brows quirking. "Well, thank you for the permission."

It was a cute interaction and Wulfe wished he'd had that kind of relationship with his own mother. She'd been a cold woman, more concerned with breeding and status than getting to know her sons. She'd died not long after his father had passed.

Elizabeth appeared to be an excellent mother. And doctor.

Noah let his shirt fall back over himself as he turned. "I'm ready to work. If there's a way for me to help, you need to tell me. And if I haven't made it clear enough, I will testify against Damon Wilkes if you need me to. I've seen some shady shit, but stealing your own son for money is at the top of my list. I wouldn't have even gotten on the plane to Florida if I'd had any idea."

Rose nodded, pulling out a phone. He jotted a few notes into an apparent text message and broadcast it. "Were you aware of the deal going down to sell the Marathon serum?"

Wulfe stared at Noah hard.

"No sir, but I assumed something was going on. Wilkes was acting weirder than normal."

Everything he said was true, Wulfe thought.

"Did you know about the senator's involvement in the program?"

Noah glanced at Elizabeth, then back to Rose. "Again, we've been there before for social events, but I wasn't necessarily in a position to be aware of what business dealings were going on. I've been Blake's guard for two years. He wasn't always allowed to attend the dinners or parties that the adults did."

Elizabeth nodded in agreement. "Damon's guard Taylor was present for a lot of them, but it had mostly been Priscilla Mattingly."

"The dead Director of Operations," Rose clarified.

"Yes," Elizabeth said neutrally. "I assume at some point they were going to do this together. Mattingly was a real go-getter. I could see her setting all of this up."

"But now your husband is following through."

Elizabeth grimaced and Wulfe could feel her distaste for the title. "I will say, it seemed like she always had an axe to grind against Blake. He would tell me any time there was an incident."

"Yeah, she didn't like me at all," the boy said flatly. "I'm not sure why."

"Hmm," Rose murmured, rubbing his chin. "Well, regardless, we need to get moving. Doctor, maybe you can hang out for a while until we check out the shuffleboard parks around town."

"I think it would be smart to keep the two of them close," Wulfe said. "Elizabeth."

She drew out the zippered case and opened it to show Rose the vial of Marathon.

"What the hell?" Rose said, reaching for the case. "Is that what I think it is?"

"Marathon," Wulfe said. "Apparently Damon hid it in Blake's bag."

"That was in my bag?" The boy asked, incredulous. "I didn't put it there."

"No," Elizabeth sighed. "I think Damon did."

Blake frowned and crossed his arms over his chest. "That's dirty. He's trying to get me in trouble."

"I think he was just trying to put it in a safe place."

Disapproval rolled off Noah, but also guilt. The man was looking at his feet, as if debating something. "Noah, do you have something to add?" Wulfe asked him.

The man's dark eyes lifted and he gave Wulfe a half smile. "I do. Didn't expect to do it right this second, but..."

Reaching into one of the black nylon mag cases on his belt, he ripped the Velcro open and withdrew a fabric wrapped object. Wulfe had a feeling he knew what it was before he unwrapped it. In the morning light, he held up a second vial of the Marathon drug.

Elizabeth gasped. "Where did you get that?"

"Well," Noah said softly, "I stole it from the Senator's safe in his office. It didn't seem smart to leave it there. I had a feeling, just from the whispers I heard, that something was going to happen last night. So, I took precautions and made sure it was safe. I had no idea Blake had a vial as well," he laughed.

Wulfe listened for the deception, but it wasn't there. "How did you get into the senator's safe?"

Noah made a motion to his ears, which had earbuds in them, the kind that wrapped around the ear. "I have very good hearing."

"Enhanced?" Wulfe asked, watching for a change in his expression.

"Yes."

Noah was a very cool customer, but everything he'd said to them rang with truth. He crossed the room to hand Elizabeth the vial. She took it like she was accepting a snake, and slipped it into the case, along with the second one.

"So, now Damon and the senator both have reason to come after Elizabeth and the boy."

Wulfe gave Rose a speaking glance.

"Yes. It might be wise to delay your trip for a few hours, at least long enough to see if we can spot Damon."

"No," Wulfe snapped. "We get them out of here. And I'm going with them."

Rose turned to him as if to argue, but Elizabeth held up a hand. "Or," she said softly, "I let him know that I have the vial from Blake's backpack..."

Wulfe looked at her, suddenly scared. "No. You won't."

"Just hear me out," she said, her eyes pleading. "We can come up with some kind of story on how I was here to find Blake and Noah found me, and maybe I can turn the tables on him. Tell him if he wants the vial he has to sign divorce papers and give me full custody. That will give you a chance to grab him."

Silence echoed through the room.

"It would definitely get his attention," Rose murmured.

"I think it's a good idea, Mom," Blake told her, moving close to hold her hand.

Wulfe knew it was a good idea too, he just didn't want her to be in any more danger than she already was.

"You guys can stake out the meeting place," she continued. "He has no idea I'm working with you, feeding you information," she told Rose. "I can text him and let him know I have the vial. I can always tell when he reads the messages. I'll have my lawyers fax me a copy of the divorce papers, amended with the stipulation he surrender his parental rights. That was the leverage he had over me. Every time we argued he fought for more custody time with Blake, and I knew he was doing it just to hurt me and get more spousal support."

Blake wrapped his arms around his mother's waist and Wulfe wanted to move in and wrap them both in his arms. The two of them had been their own little family for so long.

Her plan was a decent one, he had to admit. "How soon can you get the papers?"

She looked at him, steel hardening the blue of her eyes.

"My lawyers are on retainer for a reason. I can probably have them back within the hour."

Wulfe looked at Rose. The spook was smart; he knew that Wulfe and Elizabeth had history, and feelings, so he was going to leave the decision up to Wulfe. He shrugged rather eloquently.

If she left for Arlington now the whole situation would take longer to resolve. Wulfe knew that Damon was greedy enough to grasp at this chance. "Call them," he murmured.

A bolt of fear and appreciation rolled to him and he totally understood her feelings. The thought of her being in Damon's proximity was terrifying to him. And to her. Damon had proven that he was willing to behave like a criminal and he had guards to do his dirty work. "But you don't go in alone. At least one guard goes with you, if not more. And I'm sure Officer Rose will have other surveillance equipment for you to wear."

"We have a super tiny microphone that you won't even notice," he assured her.

Elizabeth looked at Wulfe over Blake's head and he could see the fear in her eyes, but the determination was stronger. "I can get him there, but it will be up to you guys to pick him up and keep me safe."

Wulfe nodded. "Let's get the slimy bastard, then we'll worry about the senator."

CHAPTER SEVENTEEN

Elizabeth paced her bedroom, waiting. She'd contacted her lawyers and advised them what she needed, and they'd promised to have the amended paperwork ready within the hour. Now she had to time to kill. Rose didn't think it was a good idea to text Damon before she had the paperwork in hand, but she had the message composed and ready to send.

There was a knock on her door and she knew who it was before it opened. Wulfe. She hadn't dared think about the possibilities for after the divorce paperwork was signed, but they were lingering there in the back of her brain. And she could tell when he pushed open the door and she saw his eyes that he was thinking the same thing. If Damon signed the divorce paperwork there was a very strong chance they could be together. Elizabeth found that it was what she was looking forward to most in her life. Her son would be safe and she would be working toward transparency with the government. With all that she'd done in the past two days she hoped that this would prove that she'd had no idea about the direction her company had taken behind her back.

Wulfe walked into the room, looking delicious from a recent shower. Elizabeth curled her fingers into her palms to keep from reaching out to him. When he paused in front of her he leaned down to look into her eyes, and he got near enough that she could feel the heat of him against her lips. She knew this was a test, so she kept herself still, but it would have been so easy to bridge that millimeter of space.

"You are such a temptation to me," she admitted.

Wulfe grinned and leaned in to brush her lips with his own. Once again, Elizabeth was sent reeling from the merest kiss. It was incredible. And frightening. After so many years apart, his appeal should have waned, but it most definitely had not. If anything, it was sharper. Her heart contracted as she thought about what they each had been through to get to this point. As well as what they still had to do.

"Tell me I'm doing the right thing, Wulfe. I need to hear it."

"You are," he admitted. "It's not something I would have suggested because of the danger to you, but I can see the practicality of it. Rose is searching for locations for the meetup."

She sighed, looking down as she brushed her hands over his flat stomach. "I want to get this done. The thought of him disappearing around the world and the union being left in the air, or in the courtroom, is terrifying to me."

"I understand that, but you have to be sure to present a different face when you meet him in person. Over the past six months you've grown. You were always an intelligent woman, you know that. But your confidence has grown by leaps and bounds on this journey. Wouldn't you agree?"

She thought about haring off in the middle of the night to rescue her son and treating a gunshot wound after an altercation. Yes, she had grown, of course. Some of it encouraged by outside forces, and some by her own motivation. For too many years she'd been content with the status quo. It was time to take control of her life.

"I would agree. But I feel like you've been a large part of that. When you first came to me you would have been completely entitled to be angry with me, but instead you led me, very carefully, to look at my life and my business. I appreciate that."

Wulfe chuckled lightly. "I didn't do it for you, exactly. I could only think how beautiful you were and how I wanted to be in your life again. I was *hoping* that you weren't a part of the rot."

Elizabeth could feel her cheeks flushing. Wulfe had always managed to be able to keep her off balance with his little compliments. It was part of his charm. When he'd first come to her about the drug he'd been significantly darker of mood. More somber. He'd been dealing with heavy emotions. Every subsequent visit, though, his mood had seemed lighter and the distance between them—emotionally at least—had seemed less.

"I wanted to let you know that as soon as you get back to Arlington you will have patients waiting for you. Aiden talked to the survivors. Some wanted no part of the Silverstone Collaborative, but a few agreed to come talk to you. Talk only. He said it was hard to even get them to do that. If you can convince them that your motivations are pure they will take part in limited testing."

She nodded at every point. "That is completely understandable. I don't want to put them into a situation that will do more damage than good. And the nurse?"

Wulfe grimaced. "Well, she's a little different situation. She will work with you, but since the CIA strongly suggested it so they could keep an eye on her, I don't think she's as happy about it."

Hmm. "Well, hopefully she'll settle in with the rest of my team and get satisfaction from that."

She would like to think that her people were doing good for the world. No, they were. She *knew* that. They would continue to work on the Elton project so that she could focus on the survivors of the research camps. That would have to be her focus for the foreseeable future.

But that would be something to worry about in a couple days when she headed home. Right now she had bigger worries on her plate.

As if in answer to her thoughts there was a knock on her bedroom door. One of the 'spooks' she'd seen wandering the house and grounds had a sheaf of papers in his hand. "Ma'am," he said politely.

Elizabeth walked across to meet him and took the stack from his hand. Flipping to the appropriate page she read every single line, making sure it was all correct. If Damon would sign these she would be guaranteed a quick divorce. Even though he would supposedly be getting the vial of Marathon, she'd also put in a promise not to pursue kidnapping or child endangerment charges against him. She'd thought about adding in an immediate signing bonus that he could collect from any bank, but Rose had talked her out of it. Even though it would appeal to Damon's greedy nature, there could be no muddying of the waters. If she paid him a bonus it could be construed as aiding a felon. Elizabeth definitely didn't want to do that.

She handed the paperwork to Wulfe so that he could check. It looked correct to her. But she was a little jittery, too. She would appreciate the cross-check.

"Looks good to me," he said after a few minutes.

Nodding once she drew out her phone and before she could change her mind, sent the text message off. She watched the screen of her phone. The message was delivered, then read almost immediately. Then she could see that Damon began to write, but he stopped. Elizabeth waited, breath held, as the cursor taunted her. She refreshed the screen several times as she waited for his response.

"I don't know if this is going to work," she admitted to Wulfe.

They headed back downstairs to let Rose know what was going on. The phone pinged in her hand as soon as she opened the case.

One p.m., North Shore Park, at the shuffleboard courts.

Elizabeth stared at the response, her mouth falling open in amazement. She held the phone out to Wulfe. "Is he seriously going to try to book me and international terrorists at the *same location?*"

Wulfe barked out a laugh and muttered a spate of German. "The man deserves to die."

Rose laughed as well. "Makes my job easier," he admitted.

Immediately he had several of his people leave to stake out the park, then he called a woman in. Elizabeth had seen her around but hadn't known what her job was.

"Triss, can you set Mrs. Wilkes up with one of the 529a's?"

"Yes, sir." The woman responded and disappeared down the hallway. She came back a few minutes later and motioned Elizabeth over toward a corner, then she had her put her back to the room.

The woman was petite with short ash blonde hair, a good bit darker than Elizabeth's own, and she had a ready smile. Not what Elizabeth would expect a CIA officer to look like. "Sorry, ma'am, I have to get into your business a bit. This has to go between your breasts. You have a bra on?"

"Yes," Elizabeth said, looking at the small glittering device the woman held in her hands. "This is a camera or a microphone?"

"Both, actually," Triss told her. "It's super small and one of our newest inventions. Runs on a tiny lithium battery, so no long wires or battery packs to hide. And the quality is amazing, I'm surprised to say. Better than anything we had before."

Elizabeth wasn't sure what Triss did as she worked between her breasts for a moment, but when she stepped back the device was on her shirt. She couldn't feel it at all. "How long is the battery good for?"

Triss made a movement with her mouth. "Only about an hour. But that should give you plenty of time to make the switch and come back to us."

"I don't even see it."

Grinning, Triss reached between her breasts again and tilted up the line of buttons on her blouse. One button was now covered with a small, nickel-sized brooch. It was in the shape of a flower, with diamond-jeweled petals. It looked exactly like something she would wear, classy and understated. "That's actually pretty," she told the woman.

Triss turned it a little more to show her a tiny lever on the bottom. "Switch this on when you get out of the vehicle. We'll test it before you walk away."

Elizabeth nodded, her mind racing.

Rose walked up to them and surveyed the position of the brooch. "You're tall enough that we should have no problem seeing Damon."

"Good," she sighed.

"We need to go over what you're going to say."

Elizabeth frowned, knowing that they needed as much evidence as they could get against them. "What do you *want* me to say?"

Rose handed her some lightly scripted phrases. *You've left me holding the bag, Damon. What was your long-term plan? The drug would never be approved...* Obviously that was to lead him into telling her who he had in the government helping him.

The company is going to go under because of your actions.

Damn. She hated even reading that phrase. She would give the last breath in her body to keep the company going.

You tortured those men...and in some cases killed them. (Let the silence stretch here) You're no better than the Persians invading Greece. Marathon my ass...

Yes, if she could say that, he would most definitely respond. His ego wouldn't let it go.

"Okay. I can do this," she said.

She kept telling herself that as the time crept closer when she needed to leave. Blake was an excellent distraction. There was a small fenced yard behind the house and Seben had begun to settle in nicely. Blake hated to leave the dog's side and for a moment, Elizabeth felt bad about denying him a pet for so many years. She'd never had a pet as a child, but Seben had begun to grow on her as well; a good thing as the big shepherd was now her son's shadow.

"I have to go soon, buddy," Elizabeth told her little man, as she sat down on the back steps.

Blake came over and sat beside her. "Are you going to be okay?"

"Of course I am," she said firmly. "I'm going to take Noah with me for a while, though, okay?"

Blake looked at the guard standing near a palm tree on the far side of the yard. "Okay. I know he'll keep you safe and I have Seben to keep me safe until you get back."

She smiled at that. "I will be back just as soon as I can, okay?"

"I love you, Mom. Is it okay if I don't call him my dad anymore?"

Elizabeth grinned. "Yes, it is."

"You know," he said thoughtfully. "Wulfe is kind of cool. I didn't say anything but it's okay with me if he kisses you."

Elizabeth's skin burned, even in the light of the Florida day. "Thank you, buddy," she said very carefully. "We'll have to see, though, okay? I've known Wulfe a long time but we have some things to work out."

"Okay."

As she let herself back into the house, she almost walked into Wulfe standing just inside. It was obvious he had been watching them and he grinned down at her. "He's okay with me kissing you, huh?"

Before she could respond, he stole a kiss from her parted lips, then had to come back for a second, lingering taste when she moaned. "It's about time to go," he whispered.

Elizabeth sighed. "I know. Wulfe, I need you to do something for me, okay?" Anxiety hit her hard, making him look at her sharply.

He pulled back to look down into her eyes. "Of course, *liebling*."

She smiled at the 'darling'. Wulfe had been the only one to ever call her that. "I just want... well, until we can get all of the custody issues worked out, I wondered if... oh, I've approached this so badly. I just never expected to *be* in this situation." She took a deep breath and started again, "If something happens to me," she started firmly, "you need to take Blake."

Wulfe was shocked. She could see it in his eyes. It shouldn't have been that big of a surprise, though. As of right this moment, he was the closest thing she had to a loyal friend. Besides, it was time he started thinking in a family direction anyway.

"*Warum ich?* I don't know him well."

Elizabeth looked down the hallway of the safe house and had a moment of clarity. She was working with the CIA and so many people had already died. It wasn't outside the realm of possibility that she could as well. It was time to let him know, even if it did risk their chances of being together later. If, by chance, something happened to her, the two of them needed to know each other. "He's your son," she said simply.

Wulfe cocked his head at her, as if he hadn't heard her right. Then he scanned her face and she thought she felt a wash of some other emotion roll over her. His eyes hardened, then his dark brow furrowed and he looked out the back door to the boy playing with the dog. "He's mine? I don't understand."

Elizabeth sighed, her heart aching, and stood beside him, looking out the door as well. "I was pregnant when they broke us up. I didn't realize it at first, and when I did, my parents were livid. All of their years of careful cultivation of friends and acquaintances, and I go sleep with a military man... within days of meeting him, no less. Yes, you had breeding but you weren't the heir, I was told, and not worth my time. They tried to get me to have an abortion, but I flat out refused. It was the only time I really stood up to their wishes."

She sighed, thinking back. So many years later it was hard to remember every single detail. "Damon had been in our circle. My parents were friends of his parents. Anyway, he was an only child, so a better prospect in my parents' eyes because he had family money, they thought. We found out a couple years later that Damon's father had a gambling problem and had lost almost everything. Anyway, the parents got together over dinner one night after you left and decided that we should marry. Damon had just gotten his degree and was looking for a company that needed a manager. He was told about the pregnancy, but didn't seem concerned when it came with a VP position in Silverstone Collaborative attached. He promised he would raise the child as his own. So, a ceremony was set up as quickly as possible and we were married."

She paused, remembering the feeling of being pregnant and so alone.

"At one point I asked my mother if I could let you know that there was a baby on the way. You deserved to know. She told me she would talk to my father about it. Two days later she reported that you had been shipped out and were unreachable. So, I wrote a letter to your address, assuming that at some point you would return to your family home and be given the letter. I knew of no other way to contact you."

"You told my family?" he asked, voice rough.

"I did. When I was almost eight months pregnant I received a letter, signed by your father, stating that your career could not be delayed. You were in some secret program and he promised to tell you when you got out."

"He never did," he whispered.

"I didn't think so," she sighed. "I had the baby and moved on with my life. Damon was a decent father in the beginning and didn't seem to care that he wasn't the true biological parent. It was only in the past couple of years that some resentment had been showing. That coincides with the arrival of Priscilla Mattingly, but I can't say for sure that she was the cause of the issues."

Wulfe snorted and shook his head. The Bitch in Blue. Again.

"So, does he know?"

She glanced at Blake. "No. I think he knows that something is off, just not exactly what."

Well, that was one thing, anyway.

"Why didn't you tell me when I came to you?"

She lifted a quizzical brow at him. "Seriously? You were telling me that my company, my *family* company, had done all of these heinous things to decorated military personnel, setting my world on its head, and you think it would have been a good time to tell you about him?"

He scowled, acknowledging her point.

Triss came through the door then. "It's time to go."

CHAPTER EIGHTEEN

"Sir, I think I've found Mr. Wilkes. But we have a bigger problem. The CIA is monitoring him as well."

Cameron Hall looked up at Miles, his secretary. "Are you sure?"

"Yes, sir. I called in a personal marker at the Pentagon and found out that the CIA has requested satellite time for this area. When I asked why, my 'friend' said that they were monitoring Mr. Wilkes for an investigation into prisoner of war activities and threats against national security."

"Fuck," Cameron breathed. "Get McCoullough on the line. I need to report a crime..."

———

The shuffleboard park was in a beautiful part of the city, just off the beach. On a glorious day like today, there were people everywhere. Families on the beach, kids riding skateboards. Some of the shuffleboard courts were busy but the area where Damon planned to meet was not. Had someone scheduled them time on it?

Wulfe took in everything at a glance. Spreading his senses wide, he felt for anything dangerous. Nothing... tangible.

He looked at Elizabeth sitting beside him in the SUV. The sun was shining in on her golden hair, which was drawn back into a low ponytail. She had the same pale yellow blouse on, with the camera pin, but somewhere she'd found a pair of long white shorts and sandals. She had a slip of paper in her hand and he could feel her concentration as she studied it. She wanted to get her part in this right.

Now that he'd had a bit of time to process her bombshell, he could see that she'd been in a pickle. With no one to rely on or ask for advice she would have done the most important thing to her, which was protect her baby. Damon had apparently treated them well for a while, and convinced Elizabeth he was doing the best for her company.

The man had so much to account for.

In the briefing, Officer Rose laid out a plan to take him alive. Elizabeth would walk in with the papers in hand, and the vial in her pocket. She was supposed to feed the conversation as much as she could, trying to get Damon to incriminate himself. Once the papers were signed, she would hand over the vial and back away, letting the already embedded CIA officers move in to take him down.

"The officers are there already?" she asked.

"They've been there since he confirmed the meet."

Wulfe looked at Noah. "Are you good to go?"

"Yes, sir," the man confirmed.

Elizabeth seemed to take heart that Noah would be with her. The man had proven himself loyal and strong, and Wulfe appreciated having a man like that on their side.

Finally, it was time for them to go. In order to appear alone, Noah would drive this vehicle into the parking lot, which was less that fifty feet from the shuffleboards courts. The rest of them would pile into the second vehicle and park a little further down, behind the closest restroom. Then they could scatter and encircle the pair.

It was a decent plan, but Wulfe didn't like being out in the open so much. There were towers of condominiums stacked all along the beach and a sniper could be on any one of the floors. The countries meeting Damon for the exchange later probably had it staked out as well. Damon had more than likely screwed himself by being lazy and not choosing a different location for each meet.

Wulfe and the spooks would capitalize on his stupidity, but it could also put them directly in the line of fire.

Wulfe settled into a position behind a palm tree, facing away obliquely, as if he were watching the beach. All of his attention was on Elizabeth though.

The team wore earpieces, and they could hear Elizabeth's breathing as she entered the court.

"Do you see him?" she whispered to Noah.

"No."

Elizabeth would have killed Damon if she'd been able. She was here with the divorce papers in hand and he was late. Of course. Or maybe he was just making her stand here for the hell of it, because he was that much of a prick. When he finally did appear, she was surprised. He'd been in the restroom at the end of the court the entire time. He walked out shaking his hands, like he'd just washed them, and grinned at her.

Once upon a time Damon Wilkes had been a decent guy. When Wulfe hadn't responded to her letter about the baby, she'd turned her attention to building a home for Blake. She and Damon had gotten along fairly well, though they didn't like each other much. They'd slept together for a while in an effort to strengthen the marriage, but that had seemed to make the situation more tense, so they'd gone to separate bedrooms at night. Damon had had affairs over the years, but he'd kept them quiet and hadn't necessarily lorded them over Elizabeth. By that time it had come to light that his family was destitute and he was forced to help support them, with Elizabeth's family money. It made him resent *her* for some reason, as if she'd had anything to do with it.

"Well, aren't you looking all ice-queen pretty on this glorious day," he said condescendingly as he stopped a few feet away. He glanced at Noah, standing about six feet away, but dismissed his presence.

Elizabeth tried to remember her script. "Damon, aren't you looking all... beachy..."

She let her own condescension flavor her voice. Damon prided himself on being well-dressed and primped to within an inch of his life. His barber used to come to the office to cut his hair every two weeks. It had been at least a month since he'd had it cut, and it showed just enough that she knew it would bother him if pointed out. Plus, he was wearing a green polo shirt and board shorts in an effort to blend in with the rest of the beach population.

She held the papers out to him, as well as a pen. "Sign them and we can be done with all this mess."

He took them from her, but parked his hands on his hips. "Not so fast. Where's the vial?"

Elizabeth reached into the pocket of her shorts and withdrew the glass tube. The apple juice inside it looked incredibly similar to the Marathon drug. Damon didn't seem to notice any difference, and she replaced the tube quickly.

Damon turned his attention to the papers in his hand, skimming. "Good old Trenton and Loftus. I could never get them to return my calls. It was always an intern or a lowly second-year."

"They've known me since I was a child, Damon. Their loyalty is to me, not you. Which is going to come in handy, I might add. I've been doing some digging. You're leaving me holding the bag, Damon. What exactly was your long-term plan? There's no way Marathon would have ever been approved..."

Elizabeth hoped that she had his face in sight of the camera. He gave her a cocky grin. "Well, it all depends upon who you know. As you can see," he said, waving the divorce paperwork. "And aren't they complicit, now? Since they know of the vial..."

That had been one thing that she'd been worried about. She didn't want to drag anyone else into her government issues. Rose had worded it so that they would be covered. 'Glass vial of unknown liquid' had been the description.

She watched as Damon clicked the pen, going over the document line by line. He'd danced around her *holding the bag* statement.

"The company is going to under because of your actions," she said flatly.

Again, he shrugged as if he didn't have a care in the world. "I'm done bleeding for you and your family albatross. I had plans for that company but everything I did or mentioned turned into a fight, first with your father then with the board. It got a little easier when good old Dad died a few years ago and I could start having a little freedom of movement, but the board had no progressive thinkers. They were too content to sit back and let the money roll in from the older drug patents."

"I disagree. They were thinking progressively. The Elton project and the Southard protocol both have potential long-term applications."

"No, they don't," he argued. "Old people and sick kids don't pay the bills."

She was disgusted. But he'd just led her into her next talking point.

"You tortured those men in those camps. Filleted their

skin from their bodies, broke their bones. Shot them. Some of them, a lot of them, died..." she paused just like she was supposed to, hoping he would want to fill the silence.

He shrugged, looking totally unconcerned. "They were in the military. They probably expected to die," he laughed.

Elizabeth was shaking with anger, but Damon didn't seem concerned. He scrawled his name across the paperwork and tossed it back to her. She caught the sheaf of papers, but not the pen. He held out his hand expectantly.

Elizabeth reached into her pocket for the vial of apple juice and placed it into his palm. "Marathon, my ass. You're no better than the Persians invading Greece...then getting their asses kicked."

Damon was suddenly in her face, his expression livid. "Listen up, little girl. If you think this is bad, you haven't been looking around recently. Do you think we're the only ones trying to create super-freaks? Yeah? No. You ought to check out what Russia and China are doing with government funding and support. Or even our own Defense Advanced Research Projects Agency, for that matter, just down the street from us. DARPA is constrained by morals and government. We weren't so much. We just went a little further. We push the limits, and sometimes people have to pay for these technological advances." He waved a hand at her dismissively. "This was why I never brought you in on Spartan or Marathon. We could have used your expertise. You're smarter than the people I've had working on this over the years, but I knew you wouldn't let go of your holier than thou, goodie two shoes mentality."

Elizabeth appreciated the scorn, because it told the CIA exactly where she stood. This recording would be going to court at some time in the future, and the main player had just disavowed her involvement in the clearest possible terms.

Damon began backing away and she knew it was time to

let him go. "I don't want you to ever contact me again, Damon, not for anything."

Grinning, he shook his head and wiggled the vial at her. "With this I won't ever have to."

He began to jog back to the bathroom, which she thought was very strange, until she heard a roar from the squat block building. A red motorcycle flew out of the shadows, Chris Taylor controlling the bike like he knew what he was doing. Before anyone could even move, Damon straddled the back of the bike and it had taken off.

Noah moved the fastest, almost managing to grab the flapping end on Damon's polo shirt, but it was a miss. Wulfe ran at an angle from the far side of the building to intercept the bike as it headed toward the beach. He moved faster than she'd ever seen a man move, but he lost the bike as well. With a plume of flying sand, Damon and Taylor flew down the beach, lost from sight within seconds.

Elizabeth stared, shocked. It had all happened so fast. From the time he'd jogged toward the restroom to now had maybe been seven or eight seconds.

Officer Rose was screaming into a radio piece, sending his people after the men, but she had a feeling they would be long gone before the spooks even made it to their vehicles.

Noah walked back to her. "Are you okay?" she asked.

He nodded, looking pissed. Wulfe didn't seem much better when he walked over to her.

"That was..." she said softly.

"A clusterfuck," Wulfe finished.

Looking down at the papers in her hand she flipped through to the signature page, expected to see a nasty message or something where he was supposed to sign. But no, he had actually signed it. And dated it. She looked up at Wulfe, grinning like an idiot. "I'm divorced," she said softly.

Cupping her face, Wulfe leaned to take her mouth with

his own. This time, it was no brush of the lips, it was a full-blown, tongue twisting French kiss. Or German kiss, Elizabeth thought as she melted into his hold.

Wulfe didn't let her go until she was gasping for air and there were catcalls flying in their direction. She blinked up at him as he drew back, loving the soft expression in his dark blue eyes. "Congratulations," he told her. "We'll have to figure out a way to celebrate."

He shifted just enough that she could feel how excited he was to have her in his arms. She chuckled softly. "Yes, we will."

Officer Rose joined them where they stood together. "Doctor, you did an excellent job leading the conversation. I don't think he had any idea he was talking directly into a camera."

Elizabeth colored slightly as she realized she'd just been all over Wulfe on camera as well. But she appreciated Rose's words. "Thank you. It went much easier than I expected. Well, other than the motorcycle thing. You guys don't have a regular helicopter up there, do you?"

Rose scowled. "Not at this time, no. I have teams after him, though."

His phone rang in his hand and he swiped to answer. "Yeah."

Elizabeth could hear someone yelling on the other end but she couldn't make out the words. His glance flicked to her, and her blood chilled in her bones. "What?" she whispered.

"They're about two miles down the beach and they just found the bodies of Damon and the guard."

For a moment the world grew dark, then she focused again. "Did they crash?"

Rose shook his head, motioning someone toward him. "No, they were shot."

CHAPTER NINETEEN

Wulfe couldn't say he was sorry that Damon would no longer be a thorn in their sides, but he was sorry that it was having an effect on Elizabeth. She dropped down onto one of the benches lining the shuffleboard court. "He's *dead?*"

Rose moved away to talk to a couple of his officers, out of earshot. Wulfe glanced at Noah, standing a few feet away on the other side of Elizabeth. He stepped over to him and leaned in to whisper, "Can you hear what they're saying?"

His dark eyes flicked up to Wulfe, staying steady. He didn't need to look at Rose to hear what was being said. "Headshots. Both of them. Trajectory suggests a condo or helicopter to the west. Vial is gone, as well as Damon's phone."

Wulfe nodded and stepped back. That was what he'd expected. "If you hear anything interesting I'd appreciate it if you let me know."

Noah gave him the slightest of nods.

Elizabeth was looking down at her shaking hands.

Kneeling in front of her, he clasped her hands in his own. "Hey, are you okay?"

She drew in a heavy breath and met his gaze. "Yes, I think so. I'm just... *shocked*. I mean, he was standing here in front of me just moments ago. I'm...," she shook her head. "I'm not sure how I feel."

"That's understandable. Death by gunshot is abrupt and harsh. He probably had no idea, though. There was no pain."

She blinked at him, and tears filled her eyes. "Okay. That's good to know. No one should know they're going to die like that."

Cupping her elbows in his hands he lifted her to her feet. "Let's get out of here. If it was a sniper it's hard to tell who he's with or where he's roosted."

Her eyes flared with a bolt of fear and he cursed himself. Her ex had just been shot and now he was making her think she could be as well. *Dummkopf.*

They walked back to the SUV. Noah still had the keys so Wulfe helped Elizabeth into the back, then followed her in. Once there he wrapped his arm around her shoulders and drew her tight.

"Can you just drive around a bit, Noah?"

They took off, leaving the shuffleboard park and all the madness behind. There was a crowd of people around Rose, now, and he would need all of his attention on cleaning up the mess the day had become.

Elizabeth twisted the brooch up to look at the back and flicked the lever to turn it off. Then she sagged against Wulfe.

"I didn't love him," she murmured, "but we did have shared history. And we had shared pride in Blake, I would have thought, until recently. I hope that in some part of his heart he cared about Blake."

"I'm sure he did," Wulfe murmured. "He's a good kid.

And in spite of the issues you two had I think Blake will grow up to be a strong young man."

She nodded, sighing again. They fell quiet as Noah drove them along the coastline then headed west for the interstate to take them back into town. They'd driven for an hour when Elizabeth murmured that she'd like to go back to Blake. She needed to talk to him.

The house was quiet as they were let in by a female guard. It appeared that everyone was still out on scene. Noah called Blake in from the yard. Wulfe felt a little out of place as Elizabeth drew the boy down to the couch with her, the dog taking his place at Blake's feet. Crossing the room Wulfe leaned against the door jamb, close enough to answer questions if needed but not too close to intrude. In keeping with his 'I want to be informed' statement, they'd let him know what was going on that day, but not all of the details. Elizabeth had promised to explain everything when they had more time to talk, and Blake had seemed okay with that.

"Things didn't go the way we expected, Blake," Elizabeth said carefully.

"What do you mean?" he asked, stroking Seben's head.

"Well, the plan was to get him to sign the divorce papers, giving me complete custody of you. That vial of liquid we found in your bag? It's a very important drug, and he wanted that vial of liquid very badly."

Blake blinked and made a bit of a wry face. "Did he even hesitate to sign?"

Elizabeth smiled slightly, loving her smart, growing boy. "Not really. Damon was in trouble. Our government wanted him for things he'd done to a group of military men. Testing he'd done on them. And other governments wanted the drug that he had. He had plans to meet with several dangerous people later today, after our meeting."

Blake nodded, continuing to stroke the dog.

"So, he signed the divorce papers and the government people we've been staying with here were supposed to move in and arrest him. Well, he escaped, with Taylor helping him."

Blake's face twisted with disgust. "I didn't like Taylor. Did you know he was having sex with Mrs. Hall?"

Elizabeth blinked and Wulfe could see she was taken aback. "Taylor? How did you know that, Blake," he asked.

The boy turned his head to look at him. "I saw them kissing in the pool house before dinner. And they were talking about the case, I think. The one that was in my backpack."

Wulfe frowned, wondering if the boy had confused something.

"It was just last night," Blake said. "And Noah was there. He caught me snooping."

Wulfe leaned his head out of the living room. Noah was down the hallway, leaning against the wall. He gave Wulfe a single nod, backing up Blake's claim. This was something he'd have to let Officer Rose know.

"Okay. I think that might be an important piece of information. I'll tell Rose when he gets in."

Blake nodded, then looked back at his mother. "So, they escaped?"

"Not exactly," she admitted. "They got away from our people and they rode down the beach on a motorcycle, but someone... shot them and they're dead now."

The boy didn't look shocked or upset, just thoughtful. He looked down at Seben. "I guess I'm not sure how to feel, Mom. He used to be cool with me but then he wasn't. We haven't spent any time together for a long time."

"I know, buddy," she sighed.

"Was he even really my dad?"

Once again, Elizabeth was left scrambling for an answer. Her eyes flew to Wulfe, and he made a face at her. They definitely hadn't planned to talk about this tonight. He could feel her internal debate and urged her to take a breath and relax. It would all work out.

"No," she said finally. "He wasn't your father. But he stepped in when your real father couldn't be there."

Blake didn't seem surprised by her news and Wulfe wondered how much snooping he had done.

"Some of the things he said made me wonder. And I didn't really look like him at all. I look more like Wulfe."

Even from across the room Wulfe could see the glint of humor in the boy's eyes. Elizabeth looked like a fish for a moment, mouth opening and closing soundlessly. Then Blake looked at him, and he couldn't keep a laugh in.

"I think you need to give us all pointers on interrogating and surveillance, boy."

Blake grinned, nodding. "Yeah, I know. Noah always yells at me but I know he's impressed too."

Elizabeth leaned over and wrapped her arms around her child, pressing a kiss to his dark hair. "I love you, you precocious monster."

Blake giggled and squeezed her tight, then pulled back to give her a serious look. "Wulfe really is my father, my bio... um, *logical* father?"

"He is," she confirmed.

"So, what does that mean for us?"

Wulfe's gaze met hers, and his breath stalled in his chest.

———

Well, wasn't that the million dollar question, Elizabeth thought, her heart thudding. "We're not sure yet. We have a lot of legal things to work out with the government, and there are men that our company have treated badly. We need to make it better with them and help them if we can."

He nodded. "Okay. So we're heading back to Virginia?"

"Yes, probably tomorrow once we can get the plane and pilot lined up. Officer Rose is going to be busy and I'm sure he'll want to talk to us before we leave. So, for tonight, we're going to chill out and relax. Maybe we'll order in some pizza or something. And we're going to absorb all of the information we've been given today. Okay?"

He nodded, stroking Seben.

"Has he been out recently?"

"Nah. He tells me when he has to go out."

"Well, why don't you go play with him in the yard for a while?"

Sliding from the couch he headed toward the doorway and Wulfe. When he was beside him he stuck out his hand for a shake. Wulfe took it. "I'm glad to meet you, Dad."

Wulfe's mouth tipped up on one side. "I'm glad to meet you, Son." Then he leaned down and wrapped the boy in a hug. Elizabeth thought she saw tears in Blake's eyes before he pulled away and ran down the hallway with the dog.

Wulfe, looking bemused, crossed to her. He sank down into the cushion and sighed, resting his head on the back. "This has been a wild day," he said.

Elizabeth laughed and laid down in the crook of his arm. "I think the craziest of my life, actually."

"I don't think I would change anything," he murmured.

"I wouldn't have Damon die for his greed. That's almost too much to take in... and the guard," she sighed. "But I think everything coming to light the way it has will be good for us all."

"Yes."

When she next lifted her eyelids, Officer Rose was just walking into the room with several other CIA. Seeing them together on the couch the man smirked. "Didn't take you long to move on, did it?"

Elizabeth blinked at the verbal sucker punch and sat up with a start as she heard Wulfe growl in response.

Rose paused, head drooping for a moment. "I'm sorry, Doctor, that was a shitty thing to say. I know you two are a thing. I've just had another in a series of long days and it's going to be an even longer night."

"What can you tell us?"

Rose sat in the chair across from them. "I can tell you it was a professional hit. And I can also tell you that it wasn't from a helicopter. Wherever the shooter was, he was still. And he made the shot of a lifetime. Preliminary estimates show that he was a very long way away, as in record-breaking length."

"Perhaps the shooter was enhanced."

Rose scrubbed a hand over his face and she could see how tired he was. "Yes. Which makes us wonder where he came from. And how we fight against them." Rose looked her in the eyes. "This is why we need you to get that serum broken down. If we have enhanced soldiers working against everything we do, we'll never be able to get to the bottom of the corruption. If this is an outside interest they now have a vial of Marathon. Or we assume they do. We know Damon had three vials of the drug when he headed to Florida with the boy. One vial was given to Senator Hall in payment for his help with the senate over the past couple of years. One vial was hidden in Blake's backpack, and we have to assume that Damon kept the third on him when he ran from the senator's mansion."

"So, whoever shot Damon thinks they have two vials," she said.

The officer nodded. "It won't take them long to figure out that it's apple juice in one. It'll turn to cider in the Florida heat if they leave it out," he smirked. "But the other one will be dangerous."

The three of them sat in silence for a long moment.

"So, whoever got the vials will be on their way out of the country," Wulfe said.

"More than likely."

"Is there any way to track them?"

Rose looked at her. "No. Not unless one of our covert informants happens to come forward with a lead. We already monitor the airports, so we'll watch for anything out of the ordinary."

By the sound of his voice he didn't expect that to happen in the near future.

A chill ran through her. Wulfe was strong and Noah was strong, but they were good guys. She couldn't imagine a criminal with enhanced abilities making themselves known. The possibilities of what they could do would be mind-boggling.

"We'll head back to Arlington tomorrow. I assume you'll be picking up the senator?"

Rose stared at her for a moment before looking away, sending a bolt of anxiety through her stomach. Normally he had a pretty good cop face, but his eyes shifted like he was uncomfortable. "Yeah, about that. Senator Cameron Hall is in Washington now, debriefing the special counsel about the kidnapping he attempted to thwart at his Florida estate."

"What?"

Rose shook his head. "Senator Hall claims that Damon arrived at his home unannounced, with his son in tow, but he had no idea that Dr. Wilkes here was unaware of the boy's location. The senator also claims that there was an attack on his estate, he assumes by business associates of your former husband. Many of his guards and Damon's guards were killed in the attack. Due to the sensitive nature of the charges being filed against the Silverstone Collaborative and to prevent any kind of panic, he felt it best to keep the attack under wraps and have the Secret Service deal with it."

She stared at the agent and she knew her mouth had to be open. Her jaw snapped shut with a click. "Are you serious? He's telling that story and people are actually swallowing it?"

Fury surged in her heart at the outrage. "And what about the witnesses we have?"

Rose held up a cautioning hand. "Slow down, doc. And think about this. If we have witnesses to anything on the Senator's estate, they will be in mortal danger. He's already proven he's willing to use lethal force to wipe away a problem. Right? And even if they did come forward, who are they going to believe? The senator that has served in Congress for over forty years? Or a combat vet security guard and a nine year old kid?"

His take on the situation made a gruesome kind of sense but it still infuriated her. Wulfe seemed just as pissed. "Are you saying he's going to walk away from this?"

"More than likely," Rose admitted. "I'm sure he's done it before."

Tears filled her eyes as she thought about all the men that had died for senseless male greed over the past two years. And if the senator had his way he would continue the process all over again. And he was probably pissed because someone had stolen *his* vial.

What an infuriating, convoluted mess, she thought sadly.

"So, what do we do?" she asked finally.

Rose leaned back in the chair and rested an ankle on the opposite knee. "Well, what we're going to do is head back to Arlington and Washington. We're going to take official depositions from *everyone* here, then we're going to sit on them. As much as we want it, this isn't going to have a quick or tidy resolution. Senator Hall has been playing this game for a very long time and we're going to have to go along with the flow for a while. He has the Secret Service in his pocket, but we knew that. The CIA has been investigating them for a long time, and we will continue to. And eventually something will tip the scales. But it will have to be incontrovertible. This time he's covered his ass pretty well."

Wulfe was angry, no, *livid*; she knew that without even looking at him. Her skin prickled where she still touched him. And she didn't blame him. The Dogs of War were being denied their retribution.

"I want to be part of the team that takes him down," he said, voice gravel hard.

Rose gave him a smile. "Well, we're working on that. I know you're frustrated, but give us a bit. You might actually like what we come up with."

Rose left then to handle other business.

"I'm sorry, Wulfe."

He looked down at her, lines between his heavy brows. "Why are you sorry?"

"Because I know your group has fought and lived and died for the chance to take the men down that were responsible for your situation. I feel like you're being denied at every turn."

He glanced away from her and she knew she was right. Wulfe had a legitimate beef against the world, and her, and the government, and his family. It seemed like he'd taken a lot of beating but hadn't had a chance to get back at anyone. Now there was a chance he never would.

"I think the CIA will see a weapon in you that they can't afford to lose. In your entire group. I don't think they'll run the chance of alienating you. I mean, you're still a German citizen, yes?"

"*Ja*. The CIA arranged for me to hold dual citizenship."

"Exactly," she said, poking the air with a finger. "They won't want to lose you."

Some of the tension eased from his face, and he gave her a

tight nod. "You might be right. It's hard letting go of the anger when you're so close though."

"I know." She reached out and rested a hand on his muscular forearm. "I'm sorry I'm not a bad guy you could be mad at and beat up on."

She smiled gently at him, trying to ease his mood. He scowled at her.

"You are going to have to pay," he said, voice hard.

Elizabeth drew back, alarmed at the tone of voice he used. "What? Why?"

"Because you've tied me in knots for years. I want some kind of satisfaction for the agony you've caused me."

A slow grin spread across his face and she leaned in for a kiss. "I think that goes both ways, dear. Let's get back to Virginia and we'll see what we can do."

"Agreed."

She leaned up to meet his mouth, excitement running through her at the thought that they had a potential future together.

"You're too far away."

She gasped as he dragged her onto his lap. Cupping his lean face in her hands, she ran her fingertips over his brows, then cheeks, then along his jaw. There was dark stubble coming in, but it gave him a rakish look. Pulling him to her, she kissed him like she'd wanted to for so long, with no reservations. There were changes ahead but this time they could choose their own path, no one else. And they would be able to walk it together.

CHAPTER TWENTY

Aiden answered on the second ring, sounding out of breath.

"Damon Wilkes is dead," Wulfe said.

Silence stretched on the other end of the line. "No way," Will breathed. "Are you serious?"

"As a bullet through the head," Wulfe snorted. "But we didn't take him out."

Wulfe recapped everything that had happened earlier in the day, leaving out the part about Blake being his son. He wasn't sure if he was ready to talk about that yet.

Aiden waited until Wulfe finished speaking before exhaling hard. "What a clusterfuck."

"Yes."

"So, where does that leave us? Blue-balled and frustrated?"

Wulfe laughed. "I don't know yet. Rose is hinting about something, but I'm not going to hold my breath. The CIA is running the show now. They have all of the documentation we've recorded and collected, so it's up to them when they trot it out."

They were quiet for a moment, each lost in their thoughts.

"So, about Silverstone. Where does it stand? Will it be going under? Charges? Have they said?"

"They haven't said flat-out, but I do not believe the federal prosecutor will file charges against Elizabeth. She's taking over the running of the company, and she's also going to be looking into the formula of the serums. Rose has already tasked her with breaking it down and coming up with a protocol in response to other countries with enhanced soldiers."

"*More* testing?" Aiden asked, voice heavy with incredulity.

"Yes, but knowing Elizabeth this will be very different than anything we've ever experienced. It will be completely volunteer basis, and with the CIA literally overseeing the project on site. I don't think we have anything to worry about. What we need to remember, Aiden, is that there are soldiers out there that will be weapons soon. I don't believe Marathon is as strong as Spartan but if the right doctors get hold of it, it could be."

Aiden was quiet for a long moment. "We need to get together and talk about this. If the CIA is going to approach us about something like this, we need to talk about what we're willing and not willing to do."

"Agreed. Why don't you plan a trip to Arlington sometime in the next week? I have other things to talk to you about as well, but I would prefer to do it in person. Bring your woman."

Aiden laughed. "I'll talk to her about it. I might have to pry Fontana out of Jordyn's apartment. I haven't seen him more than a couple times since you left."

"Puppy love," Wulfe murmured.

"*Dog* love," Aiden corrected.

They ended the call on that. Wulfe knew that Aiden would find a way to get through to Fontana.

———

They headed back to Arlington that day. Part of Rose's team stayed behind to monitor the Senator Hall but the rest turned into an escort for Elizabeth, making her a little uncomfortable. A lockable, padded case had been found to carry the drug and they headed for her lab as soon as they landed. It was late by the time they arrived and most everyone had gone home for the day, so she had a distraction free path up to her roost, as she liked to call it. Her current lab took up a massive amount of space, broken down into component areas for the different teams working there. Because her company worked with some of the most dangerous diseases on the planet, there was a climate controlled twenty foot by twenty foot lock box on one corner of the floor. A few people had a code to get into the room, but only one person had the code to get into the separate, smaller lockbox on one counter, where the most dangerous items were kept.

Wulfe actually seemed impressed as he followed her through the steps of locking away the drug. There was a lot of glass in here, so even though he couldn't follow her inside the room, he could watch her. The final security hurdle required simultaneous scans of her iris and her palm print. She secured the vials of Marathon, then left through the secured doors, six of them in total.

Officer Rose nodded to her. "This is acceptable."

Elizabeth guided them back to the elevator. "It is as secure as it can be anywhere. I've sent a lengthy email to my assistant. Tomorrow we're going to start renovating the Elton building. I'm going to go down and see what Damon has been doing down there. If he has the setup to make the drug, I assume he has data about it. We'll just have to figure out how to get into that data. If we can't get into it I'll launch a break-down program of the drug we have on hand."

"We already picked up the Dr. Pell he mentioned, but the man isn't saying much. He knows he was in the wrong and he's trying to lawyer up. At some point I'll have to give him that lawyer, but I have a little time."

Elizabeth nodded. "I'm hoping that once I get into the building I'll have access to everyone he worked with, as well as employees, material suppliers." Her voice drifted off as she realized how daunting this job was going to be. All in the midst of retaking her company, protecting her son, and reconnecting with her lost love.

"I'll be leaving a team here to monitor security overnight. Unfortunately, we have no idea who worked with Damon or knew about his plans."

"I can start interviewing security tomorrow," Wulfe volunteered. "I should be able to read if they had any knowledge of any wrongdoings."

Rose grinned at him. "I'm glad to hear you say that, Officer Terberger."

For some reason he stressed the 'officer' part. Oh, he must be reminding him he's part of the spook squad, Elizabeth thought as Wulfe's eyes narrowed dangerously.

Rose turned to Elizabeth. "Mrs. Wilkes- pardon me, Dr. Cole- as a part of your obligation to the men that have been abused by your husband, I suggest that you 'hire'," he air-quoted with his hands, "Officer Terberger. Technically he will remain a part of the CIA, paid by the CIA, but officially attached to your company as a liaison between us. I will also assign at least three other people to your company. You may or may not know who they are."

Elizabeth smiled and tipped her head graciously. "Officer

Rose, I appreciate your recommendation and eagerly accept Officer Terberger's appointment. He will be an asset to the company and an excellent liaison between all of us."

Elizabeth could have planted a big old wet sloppy kiss on Rose at that moment. He had just handed her everything she wanted. Wulfe working between the company, the CIA, and the survivors coming in would be ideal because he would *understand*.

Wulfe had a thoughtful look in his eyes, like he hadn't really thought about where he would fit into her life, but he wasn't dissatisfied with Rose's suggestion. It just hadn't occurred to him to think long range before this, but he could now.

After dropping Elizabeth and Wulfe off at her townhouse, Officer Rose left for wherever spooks lived.

Blake met her in the foyer of the townhouse, skidding to a stop with Seben on his heels. "Mom, Seben *loves* it here. But we need food for him."

"I think he'll survive on people food until Greta can make it to the store tomorrow, don't you think?"

He nodded his dark head and glanced up at Wulfe. Elizabeth knew what he was wondering, and she headed him off. "I know Seben didn't like the plane. Be sure to give him a good run tonight before you go to bed. Did you take him upstairs?"

Blake nodded, then made a face. "I don't think he likes the fake grass. That's more for the little dogs. He needs real grass."

Elizabeth nodded. She'd been thinking about that. The HOA would allow her to keep the dog, but it would have to be seriously restricted. Maybe it was time for a change. "I'm going to start looking for a house. Okay? Still in Arlington but more suited for us."

He glanced around. "Yeah, I never liked this place."

That surprised her, and made her sad. She thought when

they'd moved into the townhouse that Damon had picked out it would be a good fit, but maybe she'd been wrong. "Well, I'll get your input when I narrow some things down, okay?"

Blake nodded and took off running, the dog on his heels.

Wulfe looked around the space and she wondered what he thought of it. It was super modern and spotlessly clean, just like Damon had liked it. She realized as she looked around that it wasn't what she wanted either. "A new place for all of us is at the top of my list. I don't want to live here anymore than Blake does."

Wulfe shrugged and she could tell he seemed a little uncomfortable, like he didn't want to tell her what he thought of the space. "I don't think it suits you," he said finally.

She took his hand in her own. "Come with me," she said softly.

She led him along the length of the hallway and to the far end of the space. "This was meant to be a mother-in-law's apartment, but when Damon and I grew further and further apart I moved in here years ago. It is my oasis."

Inside, the space was painted a much warmer shade of blue. One side of the flat was dedicated to a small living room and kitchenette with a beautiful, glittering view over the Potomac to Washington. The other half of the apartment was bedroom and bathroom. She held her hands together, hoping that he would be okay with staying here until they could make other accommodation. Because she really didn't want him to leave.

———

Wulfe wandered the space, looking at the things she valued. He could see why she'd moved in here. It was a much warmer area, more in keeping with her personality. There were pretty little things here and there, and an entire wall of her bedroom was covered with pictures of Blake. He stepped closer, enthralled to see the growth of his son.

"He was a fat baby," Wulfe laughed in surprise.

"Over eight pounds. I felt like a whale," she admitted, stepping up behind him.

Wulfe looked down at her, trying to imagine her lean body swelling with his child. He wanted to see it in real life. Just the thought sent a bolt of need through him. "Would you consider having another baby?"

Her eyes immediately welled with tears and she looked away, as if she didn't want him to see the hope in her heart.

He could *feel* the hope in her heart, though, and he wanted to be there for her like no one else ever had before. Turning her face back to his own, he leaned down to brush a kiss against her lips. Using one thumb he wiped away her tears. "Don't cry, *mein liebchen*. This is an amazing time in our lives, because I never expected to ever have you in my arms again. So I am going to love you as hard and as thoroughly as you will let me, and we are going to find peace with each other. And someday in the future we will welcome a child that will be brought up by both parents together."

She nodded her head to everything he said, and rested her hands on his chest. "I would love that, Wulfe. I feel like I haven't been living my life fully for so long. Blake used to be my one bright spot, and my work, to an extent. But I want more. I want you. I've always wanted you."

This time he couldn't brush away her tears. There were too many. So he carried her to the bed and lay with her until her tears were spent. And then he began to love her the way he'd been dreaming of for ten years. Gentle pets and sighs led to arousing touches, growing firmer and bolder as they allowed themselves more freedom to explore. They threw their clothes to the floor, uncaring where they landed. Elizabeth arched off the bed as Wulfe's mouth took her nipple and she moaned. He kissed her other side, suckled her, until her thighs shifted beneath him. She welcomed him into her body and he fit as surely as he always had, as if he'd never left her bed. With long, slow, restrained strokes, he brought her beautiful release after beautiful release. It was as if he was reminding her with pleasure how they had been together. "I love you, Wulfe," she gasped.

Her words seemed to trigger something in his body, because he could no longer hold himself back. As he arched above her, crying out with his own pleasure, he brought her to climax one last time. It took a long time for his body to stop spasming, but she held him as tight as she could until his body stilled. Then he wrapped his arms around her and just shook, reacting to what they'd done. "I never thought I would be with you again," he whispered, and he was surprised to realize he was the one crying now. She forced him to look at her, making him feel the emotion in her heart. It was euphoric and full and confident, and immensely reassuring. Her arms tightened around him and she held him until the storm passed, just as he'd held her minutes ago. "I love you," she whispered, over and over again.

And he believed her.

———

Noah smiled and turned up his music to give the couple privacy. When Blake began to run down the hallway toward his mother's apartment, he shook his head. "Let's take Seben to the park down the block and let him run for a while."

For a long while. Because Wulfe and Elizabeth had some making up to do.

EPILOGUE

Elizabeth had never felt more satisfied, fulfilled, happy or depressed all at the same time.

The renovations on the Elton building were rolling along at a good clip. If you threw enough money at a problem, got enough construction crews in at one time, and enough brains working together, miracles *could* happen. Plus, it helped to have an amazing assistant. Alicia attacked every obstacle like the little bulldog she was and kept everyone working at peak performance. Elizabeth couldn't imagine doing her own job without the petite young woman backing her up.

Within six days they had renovations completed on the housing floor of the building. Damon had already built a dorm style living area, she assumed for the men that they used the Marathon drug on. Rather than keeping it so militaristic and sterile, she broke the barracks up into small, self-contained apartments. They were totally private and she would like to think extremely comfortable. All of the fixtures were higher end, and they were all in calming colors.

There were six men expected to arrive in three days, as well as the nurse Officer Rose had told her about, Kelle

Maddox. She would have an apartment as well, but they had already decided that she would be the one to decide if she stayed on the floor with the men she'd helped, or on the lower floor expected to be used for females.

Elizabeth wanted the housing situation to be as low key and normal seeming as possible, and Alicia was doing her best to make that a reality. Wulfe had explained about the cages and the space, as well as the lack of privacy and she wanted these to be as different from those cages as possible. In the center of the floor was a communal living area. An organic grocer would stock the kitchen and deliver fresh groceries with a call. If they wanted take-out, it was a call away as well. There were telephones everywhere in case they needed any kind of help. Rose had explained that some of the men did not want to contact their families now that they'd been liberated, but others had. In the future there would be guest rooms where family members could come to visit and stay overnight if they wanted.

Elizabeth wanted them to feel productive in helping the company, but she didn't want them to feel restrained. There were two pool vehicles ready for their use and they could leave the campus at any time, although they would have to take one of the vetted security guards with them at first.

Wulfe worked his way through thirty-two security guards, technicians and assistants who had been connected in some way to Damon's Marathon project. Twenty-one of those had been dismissed from the company under threat of prosecution if they breathed a word about what had gone on, and the rest were reassigned. Three of the guards had actually been given Marathon at one time, but it had had no effect on them. Those men had been kept on the security personnel roster and had been asked to donate blood for study. All three had agreed.

Elizabeth had watched four of the interviews, and within

seconds of mentioning just a few things Wulfe would know if they felt any kind of guilt or showed any kind of subterfuge, even if they hadn't said anything. Wulfe was turning into a walking, talking lie detector.

Which came in handy at odd times.

One of the people they let go had been Damon's secretary Mrs. Heller. The old woman had looked furious as the CIA had escorted her away, and Elizabeth couldn't help but share a smile with Alicia. Heller had always been such a bitch.

Man, I have got to stop cussing...

The board meeting had gone about as she'd expected. She'd arrived fashionably late with Wulfe at her side, as well as a contingent from the CIA. Officer Rose was busy at the time, but Officer Maxwell attended the party, as well as an older man Elizabeth hadn't met before. They sat in chairs at the side of the room and Maxwell's people took positions around the room.

The board members were too busy arguing that they hadn't been consulted about what was going on to notice the extra people. Elizabeth sat and listened to them argue about the most imbecilic things, waiting patiently for them to run out of steam, or out of things to argue about. They never did. Finally, she held up a hand.

"I have one question," she said, voice strong, into the pooling silence. "Who knew what Damon was doing with Spartan and Marathon?"

Wulfe circled the table, holding his hand over a few heads. With a dip of Maxwell's chin, the spooks around the room took those people into custody. They would be interviewed and released or charged. Cries of outrage filled her ears, but Elizabeth showed them no flicker of reaction. She'd known some of the men escorted from the room since childhood. The rest of the board members seemed shocked by her actions.

Lucas Evans slipped into the room through one of the side doors, catching her attention. "Lucas," she called. "Did you know about the drugs being tested in Central and South America?"

Immediately, his face flushed and she knew without Wulfe even pointing him out that he was guilty as hell. He, too, was escorted from the room.

"Now, gentlemen," she said finally, "we're going to talk about what's going to happen with Silverstone Collaborative. You're either going to be up for the change or you're using that door."

There was a huge amount of grumbling and some outright arguments, but in the end Elizabeth prevailed, as she'd known she would. Technically, she didn't need any of their input on what she'd planned, but they were an advisory board for a reason. Once the board accepted that the changes were inevitable and that the CIA would be overseeing their procedures for the foreseeable future, they gave her options on how to do it with the least amount of damage to the family and company name. The value of the company would drop precipitously, of that she had no doubt, but it would only be temporary.

There was going to have to be a shifting of resources, both personnel and financial. Hiring would need to kick into high gear after all the people Wulfe had let go but once the meeting was concluded and the board members left, she felt a huge swell of excitement. Her life would not be her own in the near future, but she was okay with that.

Wulfe came up beside her and wrapped an arm around her shoulders. Pulling her in tight, he pressed a kiss to her temple and she sagged into him.

Then Officer Maxwell and the other man stepped forward. He was a slightly built man, probably easily overlooked by many but there was an intelligence in his expression, a canniness that was undeniable. He held out a hand to her. "Ms. Cole, my name is Alfred Dumont. I'm the deputy director of the CIA."

Elizabeth blinked, her mind spinning as they shook hands. She'd known the CIA would be here at the meeting, but she hadn't expected one of Officer Rose's bosses. This man had the ear of the President of the United States if he wanted it. She drew her hand back and clasped them in front of herself.

"Sir, I apologize. I had no idea who you were."

The man grinned at her. "That was the point. I can read reports and talk to my officers all day long, but until I actually meet someone and get a feel for them, I withhold judgement."

"That's... smart of you," she said weakly.

"So, I have a meeting with the federal prosecutor this week."

She waited for him to continue, but he seemed to like drawing out the suspense. "Yes, sir?"

"I'm going to recommend that no charges be filed against you or your company, contingent upon your cooperation with the Marathon issue."

An incredible knot of tension released in her chest that she hadn't even been aware of. "That is incredible news, sir. Thank you very much. I promise you, the company is doing a complete turnaround."

"I see that."

His canny eyes shifted to Wulfe. "I have to admit, having you on our side makes me very happy, Mr. Terberger. You can be a very dangerous man." He held a card out to Wulfe. "Just in case something interesting comes your way or you need backup. Give me a call."

Elizabeth stared as the men shared a handshake. Officer Maxwell gave them a wink as they turned and left.

She blinked at Wulfe. "What...the...hell..."

Grinning, he dropped a kiss to her mouth. "I knew we would be fine. *You* would be fine."

She frowned. "No, I'm pretty sure he didn't charge me with anything because he likes you. I have a feeling he'll be calling you before you call him."

Wulfe shrugged lightly. "I do work for them, technically."

Yes, he did. In a way they both did.

"Now, come on, let's go. They're here."

She groaned, not appreciating that she had to go from one high-stress meeting directly to another and to another, but knowing how important it was to Wulfe, she would do it. "They actually walked in the doors?"

Grinning, he squeezed her to him as they left the conference room and started down the hallway. "They did, but I think it was because of their women. They are very strong."

"Are they going to hate me as soon as I walk in the door?" she whispered, hanging back. "I mean, I was a part of your torture whether I knew about it or not. My company provided the money. And the drug. My name will still be Elizabeth Cole."

"No, it won't. Just chill. When they meet you they will understand. Just like Dumont."

Practically dragging her down the hallway, he led her to one of the smaller conference rooms. This one had no glass, so she couldn't see what was behind the wood. She'd been making billion dollar decisions with her company over the past week, but she was suddenly panic stricken at the thought of meeting Wulfe's people.

He stopped in front of the door and looked at her. "Breathe, *mein liebchen*. All will be well."

Then he was guiding her through the door with an implacable hand at her back.

The first person she met was Aiden Willingham. Only later did she realize that the men called him Will sometimes, for his last name. He was tall and lean when he stood up from the chair, with short walnut-colored hair and chocolatey eyes, and Elizabeth realized he had a lifetime of experience in his gaze. "Mr. Willingham, it's a pleasure to meet you. Wulfe has told me about you."

"Hmm," the man said finally, before reaching out to take her hand. "Would have been nice if he'd told us about you."

The man turned a pointed look to Wulfe, but he merely grinned and drew Aiden in for a back-slapping hug.

A woman with distinctive strawberry blonde hair stood up beside Aiden. She had an athletic build and sharp blue-gray eyes. Her handshake was businesslike and brisk. Elizabeth would know that this woman was a cop without anyone telling her. She smiled and shook Angela's hand. "It's a pleasure to meet you," Elizabeth told her honestly.

The next couple couldn't have been more different. Fontana was a muscular, handsome blond with flashing blue eyes, but his significant other was nearly his exact opposite. Petite and curvy, there was a sultriness to her, which could perhaps be attributed to her Hispanic nature. She had thickly-lashed Army green eyes and sleek black hair cut in a dramatic wedge over her face. It took a second for Elizabeth to even notice the scarring on the side of the woman's face. She was too beautiful for it to even matter. And strong! She stared at the woman's muscular arms, then jerked her gaze away.

Elizabeth smiled at them both. "What a beautiful couple you are. Welcome. I'm sorry to make you wait because of my meeting."

"No worries. We were well taken care of. Although the plane was a little crowded."

A man moved in behind Wulfe and tapped him on the shoulder. She would have known him anywhere. They looked so similar, though Nikolas' hair was cut longer and his eyes were a paler blue than Wulfe's.

For a moment, Wulfe didn't do anything, then he realized that his brother was actually standing there and they lunged at each other. Elizabeth laughed at the joy she could see in their faces. They launched into a conversation in German, too fast for her to understand. She looked at the women. "He came in with you?"

"Yes," Angela confirmed. "It's his plane so it wasn't like we could kick him off or anything."

Elizabeth laughed at the remark then gasped as she was swept up into a bone-crushing hug. Nik set her down and gripped her hand in his. "It is a pleasure to meet such a beautiful woman. It is obvious to see why he loves you."

Her eyes widened and she glanced at Wulfe, looking for help, but he shook his head. In other words, you deal with him.

"Thank you, Nik. And thank you for bringing Wulfe's friends out from Colorado."

"It was no problem," he told her smoothly. "They are good people."

"Yes," she agreed, pulling away from Nik's hand and leaning into Wulfe. "I know they are."

The conversation stalled for a moment, and she met Aiden's eyes, then the rest of the group. "I just want you to know how very sorry I am that this all happened to you. I swear to you, on everything I hold precious, it will not happen again under my watch."

Aiden nodded, slowly, and glanced at the other two men. "Have to admit, we never expected to walk in here without shooting up the place."

"Or blowing it up," Fontana said, glancing around.

Elizabeth didn't know whether to laugh or not. They seemed completely serious. Then they gave her broad grins and she had a hope that despite their crazy history, everything would be okay and they'd eventually accept her as Wulfe's woman.

Elizabeth took them to the Elton Complex in a plush passenger van. The men chatted and joked around, but then there were these strange pauses.

"They're talking to each other when they do that," Jordyn told her, catching her quizzical look.

"Seriously?"

She nodded. "It's very strange, but you might be able to do it too if you're around Wulfe long enough. Angela and I have been picking up things."

Elizabeth stared at her, amazed, her researcher brain wondering what would make that possible.

The men walked through the modified dorms and nodded, looking like they were satisfied with the project. They each made minor suggestions and Elizabeth took notes on her phone.

They walked through the medical part of the building too, and she was impressed that they were able to do it, considering their history. At one point some of the glass began to rattle and she stilled in alarm. She wasn't sure who exactly had begun to lose control, but both women went to their men for support and things settled down again. She blinked at Wulfe and he gave her a charming grin, obviously unconcerned.

The rest of the lab tour went fine. The men made suggestions here as well and she diligently wrote every one down, because they all made sense to her after they were pointed out.

Wulfe began guiding them back to the van and Elizabeth

waved at the security as she swiped her security card to leave. She could do another four hours' worth of work here, but she understood that he needed time with his buddies.

Besides, she was anxious to see what had been done to their home.

Four days ago she'd found a piece of property on the north side of Arlington. It had so much more room than the three of them needed, but she assumed they would be having company a lot. Besides, she'd fallen in love with the kitchen. It had beautiful quartz counters and white cabinets, glass pendants hanging over the huge island. It made her want to bake cookies, something she'd only done very rarely. It had a restaurant style fridge, with two broad glass doors to see inside.

With six bedrooms, eight bathrooms, a music room, game room, library, den, and a fully finished basement, there was plenty of room to settle everyone in. There was even a four-car garage with an apartment above it they'd already assigned to Noah.

It had been a fluke finding the house. She'd called a local realtor at the moment he'd literally held the listing in his hand, getting ready to enter it into the MLS. The man read the details off to her and it had sounded perfect. She took Blake with her to look at the property and signed the paperwork before they'd left. So far all of their furniture had fit in perfectly, though they would have to buy more, a *lot* more. This house was significantly larger than the townhouse. And in spite of the cost she'd gotten rid of all the furniture Damon had bought. It had no place in her new home.

Seben *loved* the yard, and she had to admit it felt very private with all of the trees leaning in over it. The commute wasn't bad either. Twenty minutes each way depending upon traffic.

It was perfect for them.

Wulfe loved the finished basement. There was a media room down there where they could cuddle on the couch together and watch whatever they wanted on the wide screen.

Now that she knew her company was safe, they could truly settle in and be a family.

As the van paused for the security gate, which slowly swung open, she was confused. There were cars parked all along the drive, and they weren't construction vehicles.

"Who do all these cars belong to?"

"I invited some people over," Wulfe admitted, his eyes twinkling.

Elizabeth blinked. "How *many* people?"

She followed him into the house, the Dogs of War trailing along behind. Inside her massive new kitchen there were people she'd never met before—beautiful, damaged people. She eventually realized that several were from Aiden's brother's company, Lost and Found, and had come out to welcome her into the family.

Aiden's brother was easy to remember. He was the darkly handsome one in the wheelchair. His wife Shannon and Duncan wife's Alex were putting huge aluminum trays of something into her many ovens. Another wife—was it Lora?—pale and blonde, was stocking her wine fridge.

"Welcome to our home," she said weakly, she accepted a glass of wine from Lora with a grateful smile.

There were also children running around that she hadn't seen before. A set of dark-haired twin boys belonged to John and Shannon, and they ran as fast as their little legs could churn. There was a little girl with pale hair that looked just like Lora petting Seben with Blake. The smallest child was held by Duncan, who seemed to be the leader of the ragtag group. The baby was maybe six or seven months old, and Elizabeth couldn't help but lean over and coo to her. "What is her name?"

"Cleo," he answered softly, brushing his fingers over the reddish fluff on top of her head.

Wulfe greeted them all with more exuberance than she'd seen from him normally. It was obvious that he liked these people very much. They were important to him and to the other Dogs as well.

She was curious why they were here, though. She'd only been in her house a day and it was already packed with visitors. Wulfe seemed to sense her anxiety, because he came to her. Dropping a kiss to her lips, he gave the group his back so that he could talk to her privately. "Is this okay?"

"Uh, yes, sure but some notice would have been nice."

He shrugged his broad shoulders. "I didn't know if they were all going to make it in together. They chartered a plane to come out."

"Is this a welcome home? Or a housewarming?"

"No," he said, smiling at her softly. "They came out for the wedding."

"Whose wedding?" she asked, honestly perplexed.

Wulfe dropped down to a knee in front of her, hand going to the pocket of his pants. Elizabeth stared, dumbfounded. It wasn't until he held out a glittering diamond solitaire that she began to understand. Her throat tightened and her nose got stuffy as she tried to keep back tears.

"Elizabeth Elaine Cole, would you do me the honor of becoming my wife?"

He snapped open the top on a ring box. "*Willst du mich heiraten?*"

She nodded, her breath hitching in her throat, as he slipped the finger onto her ring. No, the ring onto her finger.

"You planned all this for me? *Us?*"

He nodded, looking extremely pleased with himself, and she cupped his face as he stood before her. "Thank you."

"I helped him plan everything, Mom!" Blake turned, "Uncle Nik! You're here in person — this is awesome! You gotta come meet my dog."

She turned to Blake. "You two did an incredible job. I love this surprise more than anything." Blake beamed at her and Wulfe as he hugged his laughing Uncle Nik.

Wulfe turned to Fontana and Aiden. "Gentlemen, my son Blake."

They blinked, then looked more closely at the boy.

"Ah, man, kid," Fontana told him gravely. "I'm sorry you got your dad's looks. Maybe you'll take after your mom when you're older."

Blake laughed at the joke and dragged Nik off to meet Seben. Noah hovered nearby, watching over them all.

Elizabeth couldn't quit looking at the ring. It was set in a platinum band and fit her perfectly. "I could not have picked anything more beautiful," she told Wulfe.

"That's good. I've had it for ten years," he admitted, his eyes soft. "I was going to ask you to marry me that long ago, but I hesitated. And we were forced apart. I had it sent from the family home in Germany as soon as we got back."

Elizabeth stared, her emotions in a churn all over again. Tears filled her eyes again, but he wiped them away. "This is a happy day," he admonished. "It is the day we get engaged and if you consent, it will be the day we get married."

Surely she couldn't have heard him right. "Married?" she asked weakly. "But I just got divorced."

Wulfe grinned at her. "And I made sure that paperwork was filed with the courts as soon as we got back from Florida as well. I've waited long enough being apart from you. And our son. I want us to be a family in every way possible."

Again the tears filled her eyes, but this time they couldn't be stopped. Nodding mutely, she allowed him to rock her back and forth in his arms.

"I have taken care of everything," he whispered in her ear. "Go upstairs and change, the justice will be here in an hour."

That hour flew by, and for the first time in a long time she relied on the kindness of strangers. The women gently guided her upstairs and helped her clean up her face. Lora did her hair and Shannon talked to her like a girlfriend to keep her relaxed. They plied her with a little wine but not too much, and by the time the hour rolled around, she was ready. Dressed in a shimmering gown of ivory, she walked down the stairs to be with her fiancé.

There were other faces in her home, faces she hadn't seen for a long time. There were a few relatives and a few of her father's longtime friends from the company. What almost ruined her make-up, though, was the sight of two school friends from college. Jana and Michaela had known about her affair with Wulfe and had supported her as much as they'd been able. After she'd married Damon, though, they'd lost touch with each other. She had no idea how Wulfe had found them or even known about them, but she would be eternally grateful to him.

As he stepped forward to take her hand, she could see the love shining in his face as he looked at her. "You are stunning," he told her simply.

He'd shaved, changed into a tux and he looked positively good enough to eat.

They were married surrounded by friends and family, and it was the most momentous day in Elizabeth's life. The crowd gathered in their home to celebrate their wedding quickly became family for the three of them and she felt welcomed into the fold with joy and real affection.

"Wulfe, thank you for not giving up on me," she told him as they lay in their bed that night.

"I never did. Even when I thought you were my enemy, some part of me hoped it wasn't true. It was why I kept coming back," he admitted. "I'll love you forever, Elizabeth."

"And I'll love you forever," she murmured, sinking into his kiss. "Now about that second baby..."

AFTERWORD

Stay up to date with my releases and cover reveals by subscribing to my newsletter!

www.jmmadden.com/newsletter/

I expect many more books in the Dogs of War series, so I hope you'll follow along on their journeys with me!

ABOUT THE AUTHOR

NY Times and USA Today Bestselling author J.M. Madden writes compelling romances between 'combat modified' military men and the women who love them. J.M. Madden loves any and all good love stories, most particularly her own. She has two beautiful children and a husband who always keeps her on her toes.

J.M. was a Deputy Sheriff in Ohio for nine years, until hubby moved the clan to Kentucky. When not chasing the family around, she's at the computer, reading and writing, perfecting her craft. She occasionally takes breaks to feed her animal horde and is trying to control her office-supply addiction, but both tasks are uphill battles. Happily, she is writing full-time and always has several projects in the works. She also dearly loves to hear from readers! So, drop her a line. She'll respond.

ALSO BY J.M. MADDEN

The Dogs Of War

Genesis

Chaos

Destruction

Retribution

If you would like to read about the 'combat modified' veterans of the
Lost and Found Investigative Service, check out these books:

The Embattled Road (FREE prequel)

Duncan, John and Chad

Embattled Hearts-Book 1 (FREE)

John and Shannon

Embattled Minds-Book 2

Zeke and Ember

Embattled Home-Book 3

Chad and Lora

Embattled SEAL- Book 4

Harper and Cat

Embattled Ever After- Book 5

Duncan and Alex

Untying his Not

Naughty by Nature

Trying the Knot

Other books by J.M. Madden

A Touch of Fae

Second Time Around

A Needful Heart

Wet Dream

Love on the Line

The Billionaire's Secret Obsession

The Awakening Society- FREE

Tempt Me

If you'd like to connect with me on social media and keep updated on my releases, try these links:

http://www.jmmadden.com/newsletter.htm

www.jmmadden.com

FB-Authorjmmadden

Twitter- @authorjmmadden

And of course you can always email me at
authorjmmadden@gmail.com

20873217R00115

Printed in Great Britain
by Amazon